Tond, Book One:
The Sons of Tlaen
Ras-Erkéltis

Steven E. Scribner

CONTENTS

Cover art:
Drennic art depicting an invasion by darkness,
the four-pointed star of the Fyorian ahíinor,
and "Imperial" Karjan calligraphy

.

1. THE LORE-ROOM AT NIGHT

Erkándas káa ílda, sellarn ii lin ínyas ke voráalis mi rényas.

Even the most heroic tale begins with a single, humble sentence.

(Fyorian proverb)

Xóa Éyuhand in South Rohándal; Eighth Month, Fyorian Year 607

A small flickering light appeared in the dark room. Rolan Ras-Erkéltis, age eleven, sat up on his mattress, looked around him. It was Arnul, his dark-haired younger brother, holding a candle.

"...wha...what time is it? Why are you up so late?" Rolan asked.

"It's a little after sundown. I stayed up. I didn't drink my *nemurath* tea tonight. Easier to stay awake. Come on, I have something to show you."

1

"After sundown?"

"Inside of course. Ever wondered what Keldar does in that room downstairs? Look; I hid this." From under the folds of his night-robe he produced a gold-colored key.

Rolan laughed. "Silly. Keldar will miss it. He goes down in that room every night."

"He has four of them. He often loses one. You didn't hear him at dinner tonight? 'Now where is that key?' he asked, 'I thought it was here, but I'm always mislaying things. Must be getting old.' he said. Now come on, let's go."

"Go where?"

"You know, stupid. What's the key for? The lore-room, of course."

Rolan got off of his mattress, slipped on his night-robe, and padded out of the room behind Arnul. "You always get us in trouble." he muttered, half to himself, as they passed the door to Arnul's bedroom and then through the gently sloping rounded hall to the stairway. The stairs led to the rooms underground, where they spent much of their days out of the burning heat of the desert sun.

There were a lot of rooms, and some whole dwellings, underground in Xóa Éyuhand; rumor had it that if you knew where to look you could find whole systems of interconnected tunnels and secret passageways, but Rolan and Arnul had never found any. But at least one room had always remained secret: this very room, the lore-room, which they stood in front of now.

Arnul slipped the key into the keyhole and massive wooden door opened inward, as if by itself. Nothing could be seen inside; but Arnul slipped in confidently. Rolan followed into the darkness and the door shut behind them with a muffled fwump.

It certainly was dark. Even Arnul's candle seemed dull in the stillness and the heavy air, and the flickering light did not reach the ceiling; or perhaps the ceiling was painted darkest black. In the dimness Rolan could barely make out a large cabinet, plain and undecorated, with some space behind it for the curve where the floor met the wall; a bookshelf, also plain and undecorated, half full or old tattered books stacked at odd angles; and a plain table covered with all manner of curious objects apparently made of metal and glass: knives, goblets, rings, crystals, and some things he couldn't name.

"Are you sure we should be in here...? What if Keldar comes in...?" he whispered.

"Keldar's asleep." said Arnul. "Now, see those things on the table? Here." He moved over to the table, set the candle down on it (a little too close to one of the crystals, thought Rolan) and picked up one of the objects, a metal ball. "Keldar calls these things mechanas; they're left over from the Ancients, he says. From before the Devastation. Here." He handed the ball to Rolan.

Rolan almost laughed. Some of the things were certainly mysterious; this ball, however, was not. "This is for playing ten-ball. If you wanted to come in here and risk getting in big trouble just to play a game of ten-ball..."

"See the holes?"

"Of course, silly. The thumb-hole and two finger-holes. I thought Keldar showed you how to play."

"Put your thumb in the thumb-hole."

Rolan did, half noticing that there was a Fyorian word "open" scratched in the metal beside the hole. Before he could wonder what it meant, a searing, eye-numbing light poured out of the ball, filling the room with clarity, rainbows and shadows. Rolan cried out and dropped the ball and it rolled into a corner. The shadows danced crazily.

Arnul giggled. "It's a glow-ball. Better than a candle!" He retrieved the ball from its corner.

Rolan's sight was returning. The light was actually not so bright; it had merely seemed so because he had been looking directly at it when it started.

Arnul turned the glowing ball around in his hand. "The other two holes; one is for 'suspending' it; here." He put his finger in one of the holes and held the ball up above his head, and let go, dropping his hand. The ball remained in the air above his head. "Pull it down."

Rolan reached up and gave the ball a yank; it stubbornly remained in the middle of the air as if held there by an invisible solid object, and when he let go it bounced and rolled a couple of inches across its invisible floor. Arnul reached up again and slapped it; it bounced again and rolled back into the corner, but now above their heads. "You can use the light to read but it stays out your way," he commented. "I came in here last night. I tried it. The other hole stops the light. 'Closes' it, says Keldar. Here."

He put his hand up to retrieve the ball again, and froze. From outside of the room, there came the muffled sound of footsteps.

"...Keldar! He must've heard you yell when you 'opened' the light! Quick, behind the cabinet!" and in one motion he grabbed the ball, replaced it on the table, snuffed out the candle with his fingers, stopped the light from the ball and apparently jumped behind the cabinet in the dark, leaving Rolan to feel around blindly.

The footsteps grew louder, then stopped, and another light, this time a shaft of whiteness, split open the dark. Rolan saw the location of the cabinet and dived toward it, feeling Arnul's hands drag him back behind. There was the fwump of the door closing as the light went out, and then the sound of Keldar's raspy breathing in the room.

And then silence.

And another spate of raspy breath, this time like sniffing.

And another silence. Rolan could feel Arnul's hot breath down his back.

Another light appeared. A glowball, from the dancing shadows it cast. Then the shadows stopped moving; Keldar had suspended it in a corner.

Silence. Rolan could feel his heart pounding. Then, almost imperceptibly, Keldar muttered to himself, and chuckled. A small scraping sound, and the light went out.

Silence; a long deep dreadful silence, and darkness. Rolan felt his sweat running down his face, though it was cold. He was not ready for what happened next.

Keldar's voice, now loud and powerful, speaking nonsense. "*Trúmiti káva mikáva ahíkulaa!*" And a blast of light, much more intense than the glowball. When Rolan's eyes readjusted, he saw that the room was now filled with the yellow flicker of firelight.

Arnul's green eyes were filled with terror. "He's started a fire in the middle of the room! He's going to burn us up, or smother us with smoke...!"

"I don't smell any smoke," said Rolan, truthfully enough.

And at that moment he felt something awaken deep inside of him, something he could barely name and scarcely control; he just knew that he absolutely had to see what Keldar was doing, no matter what the danger. He cautiously peered out from behind the cabinet while trying to bat away Arnul's attempts to pull him back.

Keldar the old man was seated on the floor, with his back towards Rolan, facing a blaze in the middle of the room. *Really* in the middle of the room. It seemed to be contained in a rectangular space, starting a little more than a foot above the floor, and reaching to about a foot below the black ceiling, without changing or diminishing in intensity. No coals or embers were visible. As Rolan watched, its center part changed into many colors and formed a scene of the desert with the half-moon above. This could have been a scene of very near their home.

"...Get back behind, you fool!" Arnul whispered, quite loudly, and Rolan felt clammy hands on his shoulders. He squirmed free. Keldar turned around with a sharp glance right at the cabinet. Rolan withdrew just in time. "Stay here!" whispered Arnul.

Reflections and shadows moved across the wall behind Rolan. For a moment he hardly dared to move, and then, slowly, quietly, he peeked out again, fighting Arnul's protests.

Keldar was facing the flame again, and the scene of the desert was moving, speeding past as though they were on a horse. It stopped momentarily at an *eyuhand* with quite a number of houses, and then proceeded to another that was surrounded by fields of towering *qenéila* edible cactus (a staple food of the Fyorians). Then faster again, now passing through several more oases and then abruptly into a grassland. A few more farms were visible in the moonlight, but now the scene was moving so quickly that Rolan could not see details. There were some mountains in the distance, visible as vague shadows, and apparently the scene was moving toward them. Suddenly it was over them, and Rolan momentarily was gazing down into a deep snowy crevasse, and then the mountains were behind, and the moon vanished behind a cover of clouds, just before a second range of mountains appeared and was hidden in the dark. "Darkness in a flame; an odd idea!" Rolan thought. For a moment the image was blank, and then an eerie greenish light illuminated a scene of mountains again; the scene was now moving quite slowly, about the speed of a man walking. Rolan could see bizarrely shaped outcroppings of rock, twisted and bent, and old gnarled trees with branches like twisted, diseased arms. A strange creature appeared, seemingly made of body parts of several different animals; a scaly fish-like body, a bird's head with a long, spiny lower mandible and no feathers, and arms that appeared almost like the branches of the trees. It padded along on thin muscular legs shaped like those of an insect; it gleamed metallically in the strange light (was it wearing some kind of armor?) and seemed to be carrying something on its back. The scene followed along for a moment, and then the creature turned and stared right at Keldar (and Rolan); its eyes were small and black; and it spat something red. Rolan ducked, expecting to get hit with venom (surely the creature was poisonous!) but the red goo fell to the ground in front of it; this was of course only an image of the creature and it couldn't have hit them. The venom had been aimed at something else, apparently, and Rolan began to feel frustrated that Keldar wouldn't show him what (Keldar certainly was controlling the scene). But then the creature turned and strode jerkily away. A shooting star appeared overhead; the image tumbled headlong towards it, ignoring the hybrid creature; Rolan saw the trees and rocks and mountains in the distance spin dizzily. The scene went blank again.

A face appeared in the flame, a Fyorian man with a long bushy blond beard. The light was normal again, and the man was looking directly at Keldar.

The man spoke. "Keldar Ras-Áelinar. Pleasant to see you."

"And you, Eilann Kun-Táninos." Replied Keldar. "But I have just seen--"

The man in the fire cut him off, but his face was smiling. "Before you tell me, uh, there is..."

Keldar laughed loudly, and mumbled something inaudible. There was a moment of uncomfortable silence, followed by more whispered words.

Surely they were talking about Rolan! What could he do now? He couldn't just disappear back behind the cabinet; he'd been seen (the image in the fire obviously did go both directions!).

Arnul had stopped clawing at him; in fact Arnul was staring at him with such wide eyes and open mouth that he was almost fishlike. The expression would have been hilarious if he were not so frightened himself...

"...so I'll bring it up at the next Council of *Ahíinor*." Keldar was saying, in a normal voice again. "A *gruntagkshk*..." (his pronunciation of the word was bizarre, with all of the consonants in the jumble at the end clearly enunciated) "...a *gruntagkshk* that knew we

9

were watching it, and a flyfire in Borrogg. Who could possibly have a mechana for a flyfire in Borrogg...? Anyway I'll worry about it later. AND NOW FOR THE LITTLE SPY...!" he turned around and glared right at Rolan with his narrow dark eyes, and at the same time the glowball in the corner lit up and rebounded through the air and came to rest about an inch from Rolan's nose. Rolan withdrew, only to crash into Arnul (who had apparently slipped while trying to squeeze out from the other side, although the bookshelf was blocking his escape); he stuck his elbow in Arnul's eye, Arnul swore and lunged at him, and they both tumbled out onto the floor.

Keldar guffawed. "Well, there are two of you. Surprise, surprise!" His intonation indicated that he was not surprised at all.

Rolan stood up and brushed off his night-cloak. "I'm sorry, I've been spying... I hope you're not angry... It was all so... so... interesting, the fire and the mountains... and the glowball..."

Arnul was groveling on the ground in pure terror. "Oh please don't... d-d-d-d-don't p-p-p-put the fire on m-m-m-m-m-m-me...! I'll n-n-n-n-n-never do it again; I'll nev-v-v-v-v-ver s-s-s-s-s-s-s-spy on you...!"

"Arnul you fool!" growled Keldar. "If you can't trust an old man any more than that, you should have gone into oblivion with your father! Now grow up!" (The man in the fire chuckled.) "Even if I wanted to kill you with lore-fire, I couldn't," continued Keldar. "I could not make my mechanas harm a man. Or a woman, or a child. Now stand up like your brother!"

Arnul stopped shaking, and rose to his knees slowly.

"Now, the truth of the matter is," Keldar continued, "spying is not good and it shall not go unpunished. (And you certainly could have done it better than you did. You both made enough noise to wake up everyone in Xóa Eyuhand!) But actually I've been waiting to catch one or both of you in here. I've always seen you two as a couple of promising *ahíinor*. You, Rolan, because of your curiosity, and you, Arnul, because you are good with words. It was probably you who persuaded Rolan to come down here! ...So I decided to give you a show when I knew you were here. You've seen the Firey Eye, the product of the mechana your father, or his friend, discovered. And this," he indicated the man in the fire, "is Eilann Kun-Táninos, *ahíinor* of Séyar Eyuhand in the east, near the Shervanya Lands."

"Pleased to meet you." said the man, and he winked.

"P-p-p-pleased to meet you too," stuttered Rolan. Arnul said nothing.

2. A SMALL ADVENTURE

Ílda no klénnas ke súrann, arn íldawal' nel syélnas toká.

Sometimes the exact details in a story depend on the teller.

(Fyorian proverb)

In southern Rohándal, in the place called Xóa Eyuhand ("Wind-Sound Oasis"), there had lived an ahíinor loremaster named Tlaen Ras-Erkéltis. He is the one who is credited with re-discovering the mechana for making the Fiery Eye, which looked like an ordinary flame (though suspended in a cubical shape knee-height off the ground) but showed events that were happening far away.

It is said that the Fiery Eye's *mechana* may have been discovered by Tlaen's friend Erlanni Ras-Tarinlein, or they may have discovered it together. It is also said, however, that Tlaen made sure that it became famous as "his" discovery and he presented it to the Master of Light at the council of *ahíinor* loremasters by himself. Whether Erlanni objected will probably never be known; the day that Tlaen presented the Fiery Eye was the day that the first cases of the Skullpox were reported in Xóa Eyuhand for the first time in sixty-eight years, and the *ahíinor* loremasters were called to help the sick and the dying and had no time to decide who had actually discovered one of the Ancients' mechanas.

The Skullpox had struck with uncommon vengeance that year, killing one out of three people; one of the victims was Erlánni Ras-Tarinléin himself, who died childless. Tlaen's wife Keláena, also grew ill, and she passed away in great agony. Tlaen himself was affected, but he and his son Rolan (who did not get the disease) both lived; Tlaen had to go through the rest of his life with the unsightly scars that often affect those who have survived.

The following year Tlaen Ras-Erkéltis had vanished out of Xóa Eyuhand for two years, leaving his son Rolan with an elder *ahíinor* loremaster named Keldar Ras-Áelinar. It is not known exactly where Tlaen went; presumably he spent some time far to the south in the Karjan Imperium or the Emb Lands, for when he returned to Xóa Eyuhand he had with him a second son named Arnul, who, like the peoples of the south, had dark hair. Tlaen also gave Arnul over to the care of Keldar, and then he vanished out of Xóa Eyuhand for good. It is rumored that he had let his loneliness over the loss of Keláena drive him to despair, and he had wandered deep into the unknown desert heart of Rohándal and died.

The sons of Tlaen Ras-Erkéltis, Rolan and Arnul , were four years apart, and since their father had vanished, they were raised by Keldar in the manner of the *ahíinor* loremasters. They grew strong and wise in the lore of their people. Rolan was muscular and stocky, with hair and eyes the color of the sands of the desert, a handsome face but with the somewhat long nose of his missing father Tlaen, intense dark eyes, and an expressive mouth that was often shaped into a smile. Arnul was lankier; he would probably be much taller when he reached adulthood. He had long arms and legs so he looked somewhat spidery, green eyes (very rare among the Fyorians) and hair the color of night; he was often described as "foreign" in appearance, though like Rolan he was considered handsome.

There was another, more subtle difference. If asked to describe what this difference was, I would say this: if Rolan were on a walk just outside of Xóa Eyuhand and came upon a nest of desert-rats, he would observe them carefully and for several hours, watching their coming and going and their bringing food back to the nest; he would stay until they were comfortable with his presence, and would remember the place and return the next day to see if anything had changed. If Arnul were on the same walk just outside of Xóa Eyuhand and were to come across the same nest of desert-rats, he would kick the nest to pieces and chase the rats away or throw stones on them; such vermin did not belong living so close to the world of the Fyorian *ahíinor*.

Seasons followed seasons there in Xóa Eyuhand in south Rohándal, and the brothers grew. It was much later that they would become legends; Rolan Ras-Erkéltis himself would be the last one to wield the Sword of Law before its powers waned to nothing. But, as was seen, their tale is best begun in their childhood days there in Xóa Eyuhand, long before the Great Tales included them.

Council Town in South Rohándal; Tenth Month, Fyorian Year 607

The next Council of the *Ahíinor* was held during the Festival of the Autumn Moon in the town called South Palms, which was a four-days' journey south-east of Xóa Eyuhand. Rolan and Arnul went along with Keldar for the journey, though they could not attend the council. They traveled by night to avoid the burning sun of the desert; and when they reached the town, Rolan and Arnul spent their days exploring the markets and gardens and back alleys of the town and stayed up late every night to watch the autumn moon come up, followed by the parades and fireworks of the festival. Keldar seemed determined to spend the first two days sleeping in their inn.

The council itself began on the third day. Rolan watched with fascination the hundred or so bearded *ahíinor* loremasters as they went in and came out of the council room every day with solemn expressions. At night, after the council's meetings, Keldar hinted that they were discussing things like the appearance of more of the gruntagkshk, (or "gruntags", which was how he shortened the word to make it more pronounceable). Gruntags were those strange hybrid creatures they had seen in the Fiery Eye. Few had been spotted until recently, and now about a hundred were known, mostly living in the mountains of some place called Borrogg. Oddly, these creatures seemed to know when they were being observed (the *ahíinor* needed a mechana to see each other through the Eye). Also, at the council they had discussed the fact that somebody there had discovered a new mechana (Keldar didn't say what it could do), and the city of Taennishland, the city that moves and appears and disappears, was recently seen somewhere in a place called Kaii. One evening Keldar looked particularly grim; and he said that there had been a madman at the council, and that Gaeshug-Tairánda had been mentioned. This was a name of vague fear out of Rolan's early childhood, when the news had reached Xóa Eyuhand that something particularly dreadful had happened somewhere in the south in the Karjan Imperium, but Keldar wouldn't elaborate.

The Council lasted nine days, but the Festival of the Autumn Moon only lasted seven, so on the eighth day Rolan and Arnul went to look at some buildings they had seen (from a distance) on the far side of the town.

They found an inn, similar to the one where they had been staying. Upon going in they found that it had a very large front room with a high vaulted ceiling. A number of Fyorians (and people from other parts of Tond) were sitting at the tables, eating, drinking, and laughing. The air was thick with the delicious smell of bread baking. Rolan spotted a round table, elaborately carved with sinuous foliage patterns, and its center was concave, shaped like a bowl, and it had a net around it to catch the metal balls which were clustered in the center, if they were knocked out.

"...Play you a game of ten-ball!" he said as soon as he saw it, but Arnul was already running over to it without looking where he was going, and he and collided with a girl who was also walking over to play it with her father (a jovial looking fat man who, from his white clothes and floppy hat, was probably the owner of the inn.)   The girl was about Rolan's age, and had a cute upturned nose, freckles, and blonde hair tied back in a ponytail.

"Excuse me!" said Arnul. "Were you going over to play ten-ball too?"

"Well, I *was*," said the girl, "and it took me an hour to convince daddy to play it with me! But I see you were going to play too, too. So I don't know how to decide who plays first."

"All three of you run over to the table and the first one to pick up a ball plays with whoever he or she wants!" said the fat man with a chuckle, and Rolan and Arnul and the girl made a dash for the table and reached for the ten balls in the center. Rolan grabbed for a ball but saw another snatched up in front of his eyes; "I got one!" said the girl, Arnul batted it out of her hand.

"Arnul, that's cheating!" said Rolan, and grabbed it. "Now I've got it!"

The girl reached back for it; "I had it first!" (and Rolan gave it up without arguing.)

"So I get to pay who I want to," said the girl, and she looked directly at Rolan with her big dark eyes, "I choose, YOU!" and she turned back around and pointed at her father.

"That's cheating," said Rolan again, but he and Arnul sat down by the side and waited their turn.

The girl went first. She picked up one of the balls, put it at the edge of the table, and gave it a push, neatly knocking two of the other balls into the net on the other side.

"Why don't you keep score?" she asked Rolan.

"Two," said Rolan, "Two for, uh, what's your name?"

"Shillayne."

"Two for Shillayne."

The fat man took his turn; he also knocked out two balls, but one fell on his own side.

"Let's see, one minus one, zero points for, uh, and your name...?"

"Just call me Shillayne's dad."

"Zero points for Shillayne's dad," said Rolan.

"What if I slip a glowball in there while they aren't looking?" asked Arnul.

Rolan didn't answer. The game continued. "Let's try this Karjan-style..." said the girl, and gave her ball a spin. It rolled around the table and knocked out three balls. "Wow, now I have five and there's only three left; looks like I win..."

"How do you know the Karjans play it that way?" asked Rolan.

"Been there." said Shillayne.

"But so have I." said the fat man, and he gave his ball a spin too; it rolled in an unexpected direction and missed the other three entirely, landing in the net on Shillayne's side. "HA!" he laughed, and replaced the balls from his side on the table. She scowled.

"Zero to zero." said Rolan, "Starting over."

"You've been to the Karjan Imperium?" Arnul asked the girl. "When? Is it true that the monster Gaeshug-Táiranda was created there?"

"Don't know. But there's a ruined tower there. They say Gaeshug-Táiranda was created in it. They call the tower T'wadzadz; meaning 'That which used to be a Tower' in Karjanic."

"You speak Karjanic?" asked Rolan.

"A little. *Chlarch'hnagsko*. I learned a little bit."

"We were only in the Imperium for about a month." put in the fat man. "I was looking for curios for this inn. Shillayne's good with languages; I could barely pronounce single words, and she was speaking in whole sentences by the time we left!"

"Daddy, in Karjanic, words *are* sentences. You didn't even learn *that*?" Shillayne teased. The fat man rolled his eyes.

"How do you say it again?" asked Rolan.

"Say what, 'I leaned a little bit?' *Chlarch'hnagsko*."

"cha...larch...hana...gus...ko." said Rolan clumsily.

Shillayne laughed. "Pretty good for a beginner, but you're putting in too many vowels. Karjanic is mostly consonants. Try it again. *Chlarch'hnagsko*."

"ch'larch-hunag-sko."

"A little better. And *tsaechbraksko* means 'I speak a little'. Oh, I know; try to say *krichpfangsh*. It means 'hello'. Actually it means 'I give my greetings to you'."

"kricha-fuffang-SKHHHH!" Arnul guffawed (the final sound in Shillayne's word was a raspy breath).

Shillayne laughed too. "I think you both need more lessons."

Rolan tried it again, then asked, "Is *gruntagkshk* a Karjanic word?"

"Hmmm. *Gruntagkshk*. Yes. It means, hmmm, let's see... *krutak* is a 'creature' or a 'monster'. *Grutak* is more than one. *Gru-n-tak* changes it into 'creatures' or 'monsters' DOING something; *gruntag* is they DID something... uh, no, it's that something was done TO them, and *kshk* is what was done. But I'm not sure what it is; maybe 'invented' or 'constructed'. Where did you hear that word?"

"From Keldar, an old man. He's an *ahíinor*. He's here for the council, and we're here with him."

Shillayne raised her eyebrows. "A traveling *ahíinor*..." then she tittered, though somehow the sound seemed filled with admiration. "They're always coming up with strange words."

Arnul saw a break in the conversation, and put in, "Is it true what they say about the Karjans?"

"What, that they have black hair like yours? Yes, it's true, usually."

"Oh. And that their warriors attack cities and then drink the blood of their victims to get their strength?"

"Ugh! That's disgusting! You just made that up to make me sick!" she looked back at the fat man, "Daddy, make him be quiet."

The fat man said nothing except, "I think it's your turn, Shillayne."

"Oh..." she surveyed the metal balls for a minute, took one, and knocked it into the others, hard, scattering them in all directions. Six landed in her father's net, one in her own.

"Five." said Rolan. "Good shot. Back to where we were."

Conversations at the other tables were getting more animated, and the smell of baking bread was starting to smell a little like burnt bread. But nobody except Rolan seemed to be paying attention; Shillayne's father was eyeing the configuration of the balls on the table carefully. He muttered to himself, "If I hit this one there, it should knock that one there, but if I pick up this one to hit the others, this one might go over here, maybe I'll try the Karjan spin move again and see if I can

21

erase Shillayne's points..." Then he broke off and addressed Arnul. "I've heard that the Karjan warriors used to drink blood like you said. But that was back when the Imperium was trying to take over Tond, and everything was meaner then. They don't do it anymore. There was some kind of revolution in the Imperium or something about ten years ago; I don't know exactly what happened except there's a half-Shervanya queen ruling from one of their towers now. It was around the time they say the monster Gaeshug-Táiranda was created. But a lot of odd things happened then. It's different now, not as mean. When *we* went to the Imperium it seemed quite peaceful. I got some curios there, like I said, including this ten-ball table, but it's not really Karjan-style; I bought it from a merchant who bought it from somewhere up north, Kaii maybe. Anyway if you want to see something really interesting, take a look at that little statue over there."

He pointed to one of the nearby tables; two Fyorians were sitting at it talking, one looked quite drunk. In the center of the table stood a figurine of a Karjan *tsajuk* warrior, about the size of a desert-squirrel standing up, carved in white wood and covered with detailed, realistic armor and chain-mail and leaning on a slightly curved sword which gleamed brightly, almost as if by its own light. The warrior wore a fierce expression on his face, as if to challenge the viewer to a duel, and his black hair was tied into many tufts in the Karjan style. His eyes were, of all things, *red* cut glass, so they gleamed fiery in the light that seemed to come from the sword.

"Wow!" said Arnul. "That's quite something!"

"...and I'll give it to the first one of you who can beat me five times a row a ten-ball!" said the fat man as he gave his ball a roll. It knocked into the others but only one fell out, on his own side.

"Six for Shillayne!" said Rolan. "Maybe I'll take you up on that challenge."

"No, I saw the statue first!" said Arnul.

"Make it beat you *three* times at ten-ball," suggested Shillayne, "I think that statue's ugly."

"Just like what a girl would say..." commented Arnul.

Their conversation was abruptly interrupted. A big, bosomy woman had stridden up from behind them, and now stood there, hands on wide hips, surveying the four of them with a scowl. She glared at the fat man.

"So there you are, Mr. Play-with-the-children," she growled. "I thought I told you to watch the bread while I went out to the market to get the food for tonight. Well I got the food, but the bread's spoiled, and you're out here playing ten-ball with Shillayne and two boys who you don't even know, and now we have to think of something else to serve our guests tonight."

"I was playing in a tournament; the winner gets that Karjan statue." explained the fat man.

"The winner gets the Karjan statue?! Some inn-keeper you are!" the woman continued, her voice growing progressively harsh. "You're out here playing

23

with the children, not watching when some of your customers are getting just a *little bit* drunk" (she meant the man sitting at the table with the statue) "...and you're trying to give things away again! You're always trying to give things away! And to anybody who can beat you at ten-ball, and you never win anyway! I thought things like that were for the customers' amusement, not to be given away when you feel like it! Now tell them they can't have it, and get yourself back into the kitchen or I'll do something really drastic!"

"...Promise...?" the fat man chuckled.

"Humph!" she snorted and started to walk off, then brusquely turned and grabbed him around the elbow and pulled him away. "That's no way to speak in front of our daughter. Now come with me!" She yanked on his arm, and he followed her out of the room with a shrug. "And you could have helped me carry some of the food!" she exclaimed as they disappeared behind a door.

"...That was my mom," said Shillayne. "At least you know when she's around. Anyway, one of you can take Daddy's place at ten-ball here. Oh, and I don't think I ever heard your names."

Rolan and Arnul introduced themselves. "...and I want that statue." said Arnul.

The moon was high in the dark sky, and the air was getting chilly, when the two boys emerged from the inn, and began the long walk back to Keldar's room.

"Now you've gotten us in trouble again." said Rolan. "If you hadn't said 'yes' when they asked us to stay for dinner... You don't even like chicken in sánatar sauce."

"*Me* gotten us in trouble? *You're* the one that kept playing ten-ball!" Arnul replied.

"I thought *you* wanted to! You wanted that dumb statue! What would you do with it anyway, even if you had won it?"

"Keep it somewhere away from you."

"Right. Well anyway it's way past our bedtime, and Keldar will give us a riot when we get home. Why did you have to go and try the Shervanya cherry-wine anyway!?"

"It was good."

"True. But it's not really made for children. So we had to sit there and listen to Shillayne play the kitál and sing that gruesome song while we were sick."

"I *liked* that song," said Arnul. "...and *you* were the one looking moon-eyed at her while she was singing it!"

"And what would you know about *that*? You're far too young. Besides, it was a very long song, and it *was* gruesome."

"*...And while they stood on that windy shore...*" began Arnul.

"Arnul, I said I didn't like that song! What'd you do, anyway, memorize it!?"

"*...The elder sister pushed the younger o'er...*"

"About what I'm going to do to you...."

"No, it says sister, not brother. Besides we're nowhere near a shore. Hmmm, I wonder what a shore is like. They say it's where the water meets the sand. But we've never been anywhere where there's anything besides sand and rocks. Anyway... *Some times she sank and some times she swam / crying 'sister reach to me your hand /And there she floated just like a swan / the sea waves carried her body on / Two minstrels saw the maiden float to land...* Oh, I forget the rest."

"Good."

"Something about a harp which would melt a heart of stone. oh, I remember; *they took three strands of her yellow hair / used them to string that harp so rare...* What's a harp, anyway?"

"It's like a kitál, but you stand it up beside you to play it, rather than lying it down on your lap. Anyway I don't remember how to get back from here. Do we turn left or right here?"

"Left."

"You're sure?"

"Positive."

"Good. So we'll turn right. Follow me."

And so they continued bickering and walking slowly through the empty streets of the desert town, and finally they saw a familiar building at the end of the alley in front of them.

"There's our inn." said Rolan. "Let's hope Keldar hasn't waited up for us; at least we'll be safe for tonight. Oh, looks like everybody else in the inn has gone to bed too. There are only a couple of small lights in the front windows. So let's hope the doors aren't locked."

They came to the front door, opened it easily.

"Not locked." They proceeded in; the front room was dark, lit only by a few small candles, and the night watchman was slumped over at one of the tables, snoring. They tiptoed past him and up the stairs to Keldar's room.

Rolan walked in first, bracing himself for an onslaught of words from Keldar. Instead, the room was silent and completely dark.

"Come on in," he said quietly to Arnul, "I think Keldar's asleep. We *will* be in a lot of trouble tomorrow, but I think it's safe for now."

Arnul walked in, and shut the door behind him with a reassuring thud.

"Now," said Rolan, "Where does Keldar keep that glowball...?" he felt around in the darkness. "Or at least a candle...?"

"I think there's a candle over on the table by the window," came Arnul's voice. "Ow, what was that...? There's something here in the middle of the floor, no, that's the table. Ah, here's the candle, wait, is this a glowball? Let me see if I can find the finger-holes..."

"That won't be necessary!" boomed a loud voice, and then the room was flooded with light. There were four suspended glowballs, one in each corner, and Keldar was standing by the door with two other *ahiinor* loremasters. One of them was vaguely familiar. Keldar

27

wore a frown, but the others were expressionless, their long beards and their robes glistening in the light.

"Looks like we're in a lot of trouble *now*," said Rolan. Arnul had disappeared; Rolan saw him cowering in the far corner.

"Where have you two been?" asked Keldar. "No, I'll skip that question now. But you *are* in a lot of trouble. I'll get to that later." he turned to the other loremasters, slowly, without losing his frown.

"Rolan and Arnul, sons of Tlaen Ras-Erkéltis, allow me to introduce Eilann Kun-Táninos and Renil Kun-Réidos, *ahíinor* loremasters of Séyar Eyuhand. You both met Eilann once, or at least you saw him in the Fiery Eye, that night you snuck in to spy on me. We have all been waiting for you to return."

"Pleased to meet you." said Rolan, bowing low to the two loremasters, in the Fyorian manner, but his heart was pounding. Arnul approached again and bowed too, but was trembling too much and almost fell over.

"We have a question to ask you." said all three loremasters at the same time. Rolan's feeling abruptly changed, and he looked up with wide eyes. He had heard of *ahíinor* speaking together, ceremonially, using the long versions of people's names, and he thought he knew what it meant, or he hoped, deeply, that he thought he knew what it meant...

"The day after tomorrow is the last day of the council," they all said together. "There might be two young *ahíinor* allowed into the council on the last day, if

28

they would agree. Rolan Ras-Erkéltis, son on Tlaen Ras-Erkéltis, *ahíinor* of Xoa Eyuhand in South Rohándal, would you agree to letting the two young *ahíinor* into the council on the last day?"

Rolan bowed again, his heart pounding, for a different reason. He was going to be an apprentice loremaster! "Yes, I would agree to it." he said as part of the ceremony.

"...And you, Arnul Ras-Erkéltis, son of Tlaen Ras-Erkéltis, *ahíinor* of Xoa Eyuhand in South Rohándal, would you also agree to letting the two young *ahíinor* into the council on the last day?"

Silence. Rolan looked; Arnul had fainted.

"I think he says 'yes' too." he said.

There was a hint of a smile on Keldar's weathered face. The ceremony continued, "Then we will see the two young *ahíinor* the day after tomorrow in the council room, after they have each found a mechana tomorrow and remembered that the mechanas came from the Ancients. We will be waiting." One of them opened the door and they walked out, leaving Rolan and Arnul alone with Keldar. The door closed.

There was a moment of silence. Then Keldar yelled, "Now get to bed!" Arnul jumped up as if struck, and Rolan collapsed on the floor. "And don't forget, you're still in trouble!"

The next day, Keldar made Rolan and Arnul a breakfast of mushy apples and sweetened oat porridge containing small chips of dried chicken liver (a breakfast for being in trouble). Then he went to the council again, and the two brothers, after they were done gagging, wandered back over to the inn on the other side of the town, hoping to find Shillayne. She was sitting at an otherwise unoccupied table, strumming on her kitál. When she saw them, she put the instrument beside her on the table, and motioned for them to sit down.

"*Krichpfangsh!*" Rolan tried the Karjanic greeting again.

"Oh—you've been practicing! *Krichpfangmosh* – that's 'Greetings to you too'." said Shillayne, then she motioned to the instrument. "...Just trying to learn a new song," she said, "I always thought that one about the two sisters should have a happy ending."

"Well it is a Drennic song, and I always thought things were gloomy up there in the north anyway," said Rolan. "And I must admit, certain parts of that song were pretty gruesome."

"I like the part where they stabbed the..." began Arnul.

"Swallow a whole mango!" Rolan cut him off. It meant to be quiet.

"I was going to change that part," laughed Shillayne. "But I can't really think of how it should go right now. I can think of something else, though... I'm assuming that you're back today to ty to beat me a ten-ball again. Arnul just had to get that statue! Impossible, I can tell you!"

This time Rolan laughed. "I almost beat you yesterday... We could play again, of course, though it looks like somebody else is playing right now." (Several children and adults were clustered around the game-table.) "But actually we wanted to ask you something else."

"...More cherry-wine?" she laughed again.

"Yes! Yes! For my brother!" put in Arnul.

Rolan scowled. "No, no, not that. Shillayne, have you heard of 'mechanas'?"

She glanced down at the table, looking thoughtful. "Well of course I've heard of them, those weird little things that the loremasters use. Daddy mentioned them yesterday. But I can't say that I know anything about them. I've asked a couple of loremasters that have stayed at this inn, of course, but they have a way of keeping things secret. They always say that their lore is not for women or girls. Rather stuck-up of them, if you ask me."

Arnul glared at her. "Do not insult the *ahíinor*!"

Rolan repeated, "Swallow a whole mango, Arnul." Then to Shillayne, "Maybe you don't know about mechanas themselves, but do you have any idea where we could *find* one?"

Her dark eyes narrowed quizzically. She answered, "Ask a loremaster, of course."

"But that's just the point. They want *us* to find one, Arnul and I, today – one each, actually. It's part of the initiation. Of course they won't tell us where to find them."

She glanced quickly at Rolan, but her expression was unreadable. "...Initiation!? You're going to be a

31

loremaster?" Her cheeks turned a little red. "...Sorry about what I said about being stuck-up..."

Rolan laughed. "I expected somebody to say it anyway. And, I'm not going to be a loremaster just yet, that is, until I manage to find a mechana."

"Hmmm..." Shillayne scratched her head. "You know, the mechanas are said to be ancient, left over from some kind of old world, before ours. They say that they were scattered around Tond during the Devastation, though I would be surprised if it would be easy to find any. Let's see, the loremasters have been looking for about two hundred years, so they say; and that means that certainly all of the mechanas that are easy to find have already been found. So that leaves the hard ones."

"Somebody mentioned at the Council that one was found recently," Arnul said, "Northwards somewhere."

"Which means that if there's another one there, you couldn't find it in a week," Shillayne commented.

"She figures things out quickly," said Arnul.

Rolan ignored him. "Actually we don't expect that we'd have to go very far. We already realized that the loremasters already have those that are easy to find. And the ones that are hard to find, well, we certainly wouldn't know where to look. But I said this was part of the initiation. There have been loremasters walking around this town for several days now."

"Ahhh. You think they hid one, or two, somewhere."

"Of course. They wouldn't expect us to find one otherwise..."

"So why do you ask me?"

"You live here, of course."

"Here, in this inn? They hid some here?"

"Well why not?"

"Hmmm." She scratched her head again. "Last night, that's when you two were here, there were a couple of *ahíinor* at that table over there." She motioned to a table to their left. "But they didn't go anywhere else, didn't even rent a room. They just drank a couple of mugs of cherry-wine, paid Daddy, and left."

"Which means that they might have left something on or under the table!" Blurted Arnul before she finished her description, and he leaped up. His feet unexpectedly collided with something orange and soft and furry, and he sprawled onto the floor. Rolan laughed. The furry thing let out a yelp and a meow, and jumped up onto Shillayne's lap.

"Are you all right?" She asked.

Arnul sat up, but looked ready to cry. "...I think so..." he muttered.

"Not you! I meant the cat!" said Shillayne. Rolan's laughter reached a howl. Shillayne introduced the cat as Whiskers, and stroked its back until it started to purr, evidently unfazed by Arnul's clumsiness. Rolan continued to laugh, much to Arnul's consternation; finally the younger boy stood up and aimed a fist at Rolan. Rolan ducked, and Shillayne said, "Be careful!

33

You'll upset the cat here. Besides if you start fighting, I'll go over there and get that hidden mechana myself!"

"Aha, so you're admitting that you know there is one there!" said Rolan. He made a move toward the table; Arnul tripped him and he clumsily sprawled onto the floor. This time Shillayne guffawed, and the cat ran away.

Rolan stood. "Truce?"

"Truce." Said Arnul.

"Good. Now let's go look together – it shouldn't be this difficult to go halfway across a room to another table!"

The three of them ran over to the other table. It was, of course, an ordinary table much like the one they had just been sitting at. Round, made of wood, supported by four wooden legs; there was an unlit candle sitting on it and two chairs next to it. There was nothing else, sitting on it or near it, or stuck somehow to its underside or legs.

"Boring!" said Arnul.

"Not here – that leaves everywhere else in this inn," said Shillayne. "We could go and look in every room, of course, though there aren't any loremasters staying here right now..."

Rolan interrupted. "Actually, I don't think they'd put it anywhere here anyway; and certainly not anywhere in plain sight like on this table. I think they probably hid it somewhere that looks more mysterious – you know how they are always trying to look mysterious. And of course they hid it, not just put it somewhere. Is there a place in this town, like a tunnel or a secret passage or something…?"

"Well if it's too secret I certainly wouldn't know about it! But of course there are always those stories. 'Anywhere that Fyorians build, there are hidden doors and passageways underground…' I know of one near here. It goes from under the street to out near the Tombs; there are some farms out there and the farmers used to stash extra grain there to keep from paying tax to the Master of Light. There's another tunnel over on the other side of town, but I don't know where it goes."

Arnul was scratching his head. "Tombs!" He said suddenly. "How old are they?"

"From the Ancients."

Rolan raised an eyebrow. "Well, for once you figured out a clue quicker to me! Keldar did say to remember that the mechanas came from the Ancients. Shillayne, could you show us the passageway?"

"Well – no, not really. I have to go to school today, and I'm supposed to stay here to help mommy and daddy anyway, and besides, they'd get upset about me leaving with a couple of boys. …But, I could tell you where it is."

"That would do," said Rolan.

Shillayne gave a mischievous smile. "You'll each have to play me a game of ten-ball first," she said, and motioned to the game-table; there were still several other children playing the game.

"We're next!" Arnul said.

It was the hot part of the mid afternoon when the two boys came to the street that Shillayne had described. On the left side of the street, there was the house with red-orange adobe and a garden in front that seemed to be growing mostly flowers. On the right side, there was the small shop with the elaborately carved wooden sign reading

Small Items from Woodworkers Shémilar and Túnlei: wooden bowls and eating utensils; walking-staffs and canes, small cabinets and racks; gameboards, curios and knick-knacks. Rare and interesting wood imported from Kaii, the Drennlands, the Karjan Imperium and the Emb Lands.

"Well, this looks like the place." Said Rolan. "She mentioned the wood-shop and the flower-garden. The doorway should be behind the house with the flower garden, behind the gate."

And surely enough, there was a dirt path leading beside the house with the bright adobe, which went up to a wooden fence. There was a gate in the exact middle, taller than either of them and arched overhead. It was made of slats carved with scenes of foliage, with one odd section painted in several wide stripes of blue, brown, and white; undulating horizontal lines, perhaps made from the wood-grain itself. Some of the paint had chipped off.

"Hmmm, she mentioned a part of the gate made from some old northern Tondish art that had been reclaimed. I think this painted part must be that, so now I'm certain that this is the right place." Said Rolan.

"She also mentioned that you couldn't see behind on one side of the fence." Said Arnul, peering closely at the wooden slats on the left side. "I can see through here – there's another garden behind. Must be the other side."

"It is." Rolan replied; he strained to look through the boards on the other side, the right side, but could see nothing but blackness behind.

"This is it," said Rolan. "Shall we go in?" Arnul stared at him. "That's why we're here, stupid." Rolan ignored him and rattled the gate with his hands. It did not move. He looked for a lock or latch, but could find nothing.

"Well it certainly is secret." Said Arnul. "Anybody trying to get in would think that the gate must only be for decoration, and it doesn't really move at all. Do you think Shillayne really knew there was a passage here?" Rolan did not answer, so he continued, "Of course, we could just kick it in."

"No, look." Rolan said suddenly. He had been feeling along the bottom edge of the gate, carefully, to avoid splinters. His hand touched a small metal protrusion.

"Just a nail." Arnul said confidently.

"Nails don't move like this." Said Rolan, and he pulled on it. Click. Something unlocked, and the gate swung open inwards, towards the right. He went in, and Arnul shrugged and followed. Rolan shut the gate behind them.

They did not seem to have entered a secret passageway. The house with red-orange adobe continued back on their left for about twenty feet, back to what seemed to be another street. The wood-shop building was about the same size. Between them was a garden, and several pumpkin plants were growing in the tilled soil; one had a small but ripe pumpkin. The air was still and much hotter than outside of the gate.

There was a door to their right, made of weathered wooden slats like the gate, though it appeared to be much older. Words were painted directly on it in shiny black; they were not weathered so they had probably been made recently.

Kéyn gárnyasen (DO NOT ENTER)

"I'll assume it's misspelled," said Rolan ("Please enter" would only have one letter different in Fyorian), and he pushed on the door. Again, it was locked solid. It would not budge.

"Again, I'll say we could kick it in," said Arnul.

Rolan stared at him and wrinkled an eyebrow; then he turned away and felt along the wood of the door.

There was no underside. It came right to the floor and there was not enough room to get his fingers underneath, and the edges were also tight against the walls. He ran his fingertips along the front. Not quite carefully enough; he pulled back with a yelp and pulled a half-inch sliver from his finger. No blood; it just smarted a little.

"*You* try looking for something," he said to Arnul.

"It's probably over there," said Arnul, pointing to five nails driven into the side of the wood-shop building, in a vertical straight line; Rolan had not noticed them before. Arnul pulled on one of the nails, and of course it did not budge. "Maybe not," he said.

"There are five of them. Why give up after just one?"

"Hmmm..." Arnul tried to move the bottom nail in the line; it was just as solid. So were the other three.

"You don't suppose you have to know some of those formulae that the loremasters say," said Rolan. "Like when they use their mechanas. This lock could be a mechana of some kind! Or..." He had had another idea, and he stepped over to the nails, but then stooped over to inspect the grassy ground closely. It was overgrown with weeds.

"What are you looking for?"

"This." He replied, pointing to a shallow square indentation in the ground. Not a natural shape for dirt or grass to assume. Rolan put his foot on it, and it sunk slightly deeper. Then, clunk, something slipped inside of the wall.

"Now try the nails," he said.

Arnul grabbed the top nail again. Still it did not budge. He tried the second, again with no results. He tried the third, and it pulled slightly upwards. The same for the fourth. The fifth would not move, but he tried the first again, and there was another click.

Rolan pushed on the door, and it swung open. There were stairs behind it, leading down into darkness. Rolan stepped in; Arnul stayed back. "Maybe this is where we go back." He said.

Rolan stared at him from inside the doorway. "Do you want to be a loremaster or not...?"

Arnul hesitated, then scowled and walked in, glancing around fearfully. Rolan stepped in front of him and said, "Remember — it was you who led me into Keldar's lore room that night!"

"True enough!" said Arnul, suddenly meeting Rolan's stare, and then he pushed his brother aside and descended three steps. He turned around. "Are you sure?"

Rolan rolled his eyes and almost laughed. "We'll go together," he said, holding Arnul's hand. He didn't really want to admit that he was beginning to feel a little frightened himself.

The stairs were steep and irregular, made of cold gray stone, and difficult to see. The two of them felt ahead with their feet to make sure that each next step was solid, and proceeded. Down, into underground; the walls around them were also made of gray stone. The light from the doorway slowly became dimmer and then seemed to vanish altogether. Here they paused, waiting for their eyes to adjust (Rolan could feel Arnul trembling slightly); but after a couple of minutes they decided that they weren't going to be able to see any better.

Rolan nudged Arnul to pull the glowball (Keldar's) from out of his pocket, which he shakily did. He handed it to Rolan, who put his finger in the fingerhole, "opening" the light.

Now they could see. The walls and stairs were not only of irregular gray stone, but they were actually crumbling in places, and cracks were visible in all directions, filled with dirt. There was another wall directly in front of them, and the stairs bent to the right.

Rolan peered around the bend, and saw that the stairs came to a flat hallway, which continued more or less straight as far as the glowball cast its light. He pulled Arnul with him, and stepped down the last three stairs.

The walls, ceiling, and floors were all of the same kind of stone, and the passage was just wide enough for the two of them to walk side by side, though the ceiling arched several feet over their heads. The air was becoming musty, and there were more cracks in the stone; but no fallen rocks blocked their way. Rolan suspended the glowball slightly above eye level, and rolled it ahead. The passage continued straight for some time; they caught up to the glowball and rolled it ahead again.

Rolan could not be sure exactly how long they continued in this manner. The hall was seemingly endless, and monotonous; Rolan kept expecting to see something different – a different kind of stone in the walls or floor, a little recessed area, a section that was severely cracked and pockmarked. But nothing changed. He decided that he would even welcome the sight of a mouse or rat (such things lived in places like this, of course), but there was not movement or sound besides their heavy footprints.

Finally Arnul said, "This is awful! We've been in here for two hours. How do we even know if we're going the right way, and how do we even know that if we turn back, the gate will still be open? And can we open it from the inside, if it's not!?" Rolan jumped at his sudden speech, so loud there in the still air, and he could see panic beginning in Arnul's eyes. He didn't feel so sure himself, though he was certain that it had been a lot less than two hours. All he could say was, "Well don't back out now! We've already come this far!" He grabbed Arnul by the shoulder and pushed him ahead slightly, trying to act braver than he was. Arnul froze, then reluctantly took another step. Rolan followed.

They caught up to the glowball again, and Rolan rolled it forward.

And saw something different.

Finally.

"I think that's the end!" He said, quite loudly, both so Arnul could hear it and so he could hear himself say it. There was an arch-shaped darkness up there; when they caught up the found that the hall branched like a T into two directions, both which seemed to ascend rapidly, though the light from the glowball was rather feeble and could not penetrate far into the shadows in either direction.

"...Well?" said Arnul.

Rolan sniffed the air. Certainly it was fresher now than it had been; the earthy smell was replaced by dry air with hints of flowers and grasses. The aroma was slightly stronger from the left than the right.

"I guess the left side goes up to the surface." He said. "So the right side might be where they could hide something, but I think some fresh air would be good first. Let's go to the left."

Arnul agreed, and bounded ahead into the darkness, and screamed.

It took Rolan a second to recover. Then he ran forward as well, grabbing the glowball as he went. He found Arnul just a few steps ahead, cowering nearly on the floor, and there were steps going up just beyond him. He could see nothing else.

"What happened?"

Arnul was visibly shaken, but he tried to stand. "N-n-n-nothing really... Just those cobwebs... almost scared me out of Tond!"

Rolan nearly slapped him. "I thought I had to rescue you from something!" he snapped, and he muttered (loud enough for Arnul to hear), "Where's a real monster when you need one!?"

But the ceiling was full of hanging webs, now that he looked more closely — nearly invisible, threadlike, and hanging nearly to his waist. They began about where Arnul was, and continued up to the edge of the stairs, and maybe beyond.

Rolan took the glowball down from its position at eye level, and rolled it to the stairs. The moving luminescence made the webs stand out like thin lines of light and shadow, which bent and swayed in the slightly moving air. Rolan mused that cobwebs were nothing to be afraid of, but it would be terrible if they were actually living tentacles from some creature hiding behind the wall or ceiling. Not that such a thing was likely, but the thought unnerved him.

Arnul had recovered by now, and he went first towards the stairs, crouching to avoid the hanging strings. Rolan followed, and he was relieved that none of them tried to grab him. The boys reached the stairs quickly, and started up.

The air grew fresher almost immediately, and soon light was visible. Not the shadowy, shifting light from the glowball, but the golden-white radiance of daylight. And in another minute, they had stepped out of the tunnel – the stairs simply continued right up to the surface.

Rolan's courage was returning. He blinked and shielded his eyes from the sunlight. He could see nothing at first because of the glare, but he was quite certain that it was not yet evening (they hadn't been in the passage very long at all!); even if the sunlight had not been so bright, the heat of the desert day was still oppressive.

Their eyes began to adjust. They were standing on the edge of the town, so it appeared; in front of them were the sands and scrub of the desert, stretching off towards the horizon. Behind them were buildings, small scruffy-looking shacks and lean-tos, the kind used for storage and sometimes found near the edges of Fyorian towns. And to their left was something (shimmering in the heat) that looked like much larger buildings, possibly of stone.

"That would be the Tombs." Rolan said.

"...But they're out there in the sand! We can't go that far out; there are poisonous snakes out there!" Arnul objected.

"There are also those delicious edible cactuses out there. Besides, I don't know if we have to go out there or not. Nobody ever said anything about where our mechana might be. It was only a guess, and a hint from Keldar. Maybe we should poke around here for clues first, if they aren't back down in that other underground room."

He began to look along the ground, though of course he was not entirely sure of what he might find. Arnul joined him, sweating, either from the suddenly hot air or fear of going out to the tombs.

It was not long before their search was rewarded. Arnul saw them first – footprints, leading from near the emergence of the stairs, towards the nearer shacks. He pointed them out to Rolan, and the two of them followed. The trail was half-obscured in some places by

45

wind-blown sand and dirt, but it appeared to be fairly fresh.

Right up next to a wooden lean-to, the prints disappeared. Rolan had been so intent on keeping his eyes on them that he didn't stand up when they ended (he kept looking around at the ground) and nearly crashed into the stone pillar. As it was, he saw its stone base, and looked up just in time to step not-very-nimbly out of the way, and he nearly tripped. Arnul giggled (he was obviously beginning to feel more confident). "I tripped you in the inn, but you're getting worse – how could s stone pole trip you!?"

"Swallow a whole mango," was all Rolan could say. The pillar was an obvious marker for something, though he didn't know what, and (ignoring Arnul's continued snickering) he examined it. It was made of marble, so it looked, rather expensive and heavy material; it was probably a foot thick, square in the cross-section (or vaguely trapezoidal), and about seven feet tall. He couldn't see if there was (or had been) anything on top of it, but one side was decorated with carved symbols. He couldn't make them out at first, until he got to exactly the right place and the sun shone onto it from just the right angle. Then he could read them as Fyorian letters:

Council Eyuhand and grand cavern
Established at South Palms
In the 3rd year of the Reign of Master of Light
Túrath Ras-Xéldusan

As meeting place for the Council of Ahíinor every five years.

And it continued with a long name of dates and names, history of the town.

"It's probably interesting," said Rolan, "if we were to come here later when it's cooler, and if we knew something about these people. But for now it's just a place-marker; tells us nothing about our mechana."

Arnul had quit smirking. "But the footprints led right up to it, and we can probably assume that they were Keldar's prints, because they were recent." He said.

"But they could be somebody else's – how secret can this place really *be*?" Rolan asked; but all the same he examined the ground to see if the same footprints led away from the pillar in a different direction. He couldn't see any except two or three that seemed to retrace the first set and then disappear into the sand, by two tall sticks that had been shoved into the ground vertically.

"If they're Keldar's prints, then this is the place." He said.

"Hey – Look over here." Said Arnul, pointing to another side of the pillar.

Rolan peered around to the other side, and saw more writing. Not carvings, they were smeared on the stone with what appeared to be soap. They were barely visible, and he had completely overlooked them before.

Brothers Ras-Erkéltis,
Congradulations.
You have found your walking-staffs.

"Well, this is the right place!" exclaimed Rolan, and then, "...but of course it's *not*; because this is telling us something about walking-staffs, not mechanas, and I certainly don't know anything about..."

His words trailed off. Both he and Arnul stared at the sticks in the ground; each was about as tall as a man, and each was slightly bent and knobby and made of darkwood. They were like the staffs carried by the *ahíinor*. And the staffs carried by the *ahíinor* were mechanas, it was said.

3. THE INITIATION

Ahíinráalis nel vórn arn tán ni xéndadhas.
The words of the *ahiinor* are carved in stone.
(From the annals of the *ahíinor*)

Council Town in South Rohándal; Tenth Month, Fyorian Year 607

Sleep eluded Rolan that night as he lay on his mattress, anxious and fearful about the next day. What would the *ahíinor* do to him tomorrow? He had heard hints that there was a ceremony of special grandeur, but he had also heard tales of fear and pain. The *ahíinor* did not take their position lightly; and to join their ranks, one would have to take some kind of test. Undoubtedly they would not hurt him physically, but there were other ways, such as the *mechanas* themselves, to induce pain. Holding extremely bright glowballs up to one's eyes, for example, or using the Fiery Eye to show scenes of something horrible; what, he couldn't imagine. They would do... they would do... no, he dared not think of what they would do; but he knew that he must do it with them. Such had been his desire since he had seen Keldar look through the Fiery Eye and see the realms of Tond. Something had awoken within him then, and he knew that he would have to walk the path to become an *ahíinor*. There was no other path to take.

So he lay there, tired but wide awake, and watched the stars from his window; the constellation of the Scimitar set in the west, and the Hourglass began to rise when the first rosy light of dawn appeared in the east. He felt Keldar gently wake him.

He sat up and rubbed his eyes. "I didn't realize I was asleep." he yawned. "Is Arnul up yet?"

Keldar didn't answer, but walked out of the room slowly. So one had to be quiet on the day of initiation.

Rolan stretched. His muscles twanged and he realized he was sore from the adventure the day before and the almost sleepless night. He got up, went to the wardrobe, got his tunic and put it on, waited a minute, took a deep breath, grabbed his new walking-staff, and proceeded out of the room to join Keldar. Arnul was already up, and was eating some grapes from the bunch that Shillayne had given them the night before. Rolan's stomach was too unquiet to have any. Keldar stood there and observed them both with his narrow eyes;

then he took his own *árukand* walking-staff, threw the door open, and walked out into the light of the rising sun. Rolan followed slowly, Arnul bounced out of the door behind him, shut it, and bounded ahead.

The morning air was crisp, but already the heat of the desert sun was beginning to make itself known. In another two hours the air would be hot and stifling, but for now it was comfortable and there were some birds singing. Rolan heard them as they passed. A stray dog sniffed at their heals, then crossed behind them as they walked down the narrow cobbled streets, but there was no other sound. Nobody was out yet this morning;. They passed the marketplace where usually there were throngs of people and the air was scented with the strong smells of fruits and animals and spices and sweat. This morning there were no people, and the only smell was an occasional pine or flower as they passed.

"Where *is* everybody?" he asked, mostly to himself. He started; his own voice had been loud and harsh.

"It is two days after the Festival of the Autumn Moon." Said Keldar abruptly but quietly. "This town has a Day of Silence to be thankful for the harvest. Nobody works on this day." He gestured to show that they should obey the custom too, but then he said quietly, "The Council will be very noisy, but it will be inside. We will not disturb their silence."

And so they walked silently to the Council Building, and there they met the hundred or so bearded

51

loremasters, standing in a barely organized crowd outside of the door; all leaning on *árukand* walking-staffs, and all observing Rolan and Arnul solemnly. Rolan recognized Eilann among them. He alone was smiling.

There was another *ahíinor* in a large red and blue robe, quite unlike the drab ones the others were wearing, and his walking-staff was not knobby but straight, carved with foliage patterns, and topped with a gold ornament shaped like a four-pointed star. He was the leader, the *lúmukor*, the Master of Light, whom Keldar had spoken of. He regarded Rolan and Arnul each in turn with a long steady gaze, then waved his walking-staff in the air, opened the door, and went in. The others followed, with Rolan, Arnul and Keldar in the rear.

Rolan immediately realized he had actually never seen the inside of this building. The *outside* certainly was unimpressive; a rather haphazard structure of boards nailed together and partially covered with old, wearing-off adobe; but it was usual for the Fyorians not to worry much about the appearance of the outside of a building. As they passed under the doorway, Rolan deliberately gazed around at the inside, but at first he could see very little; there were only a few glowballs and candles placed in stands along the walls to provide light, and it was quite dim. At least he could be certain that they were walking down some kind of a hallway. The air was thick and oppressive. Presently the floor began to slope downward, gently at first, and then much more steeply. There was a railing on the wall now.

For several minutes they padded onward in silence, the only sounds from the shuffling of their feet (and Rolan's pounding heart, he was sure). They came to a very dark place; there were no glowballs or candles at all; to Rolan the darkness looked almost like a wall, and the *ahíinor* simply seemed to disappear into it. Nothing could be seen further in, except vague shadows of the loremasters themselves and some dim lights that looked unusually small. He hesitated before the yawning blackness, noticed that Arnul was also standing there terrified. He took a deep breath (the air was vaguely damp now) and proceeded in.

He saw the inside and almost dropped to the ground. They were entering a cavern, a cavern of such dimensions that the far wall and the ceiling were lost in the shadows, and the floor sloped away into nothingness. ...And to think that this immense hall had been under their feet, unknown, the whole time they had been in this town!

For a moment he stood there in awe, until Keldar nudged him with his walking-staff and motioned to his side. There were the other *ahíinor*, seated; Rolan noticed now that there were benches in this part of the cavern. He could barely move, still, but Keldar kept nudging him to sit down. Finally he tore his eyes away from the void surrounding him, and he took his seat on the nearest bench. It was not wood, as he had expected, but stone, cold and hard, as if carved out of the very rock of the cavern. Keldar sat down beside him, and he could also dimly make out in the gloom that Arnul had taken a seat on the other side of Keldar, and was sitting there sullenly, probably terrified, no longer wanting to jump or bound around.

And then, in a soundless explosion of darkness, all the lights went out.

Rolan caught his breath. Were they going to leave him here in the darkness? Was that part of the trial? Or was the whole Council going to take place unseen? At any rate the darkness was seamless and complete; darker than the darkest night, for here underground there could be no stars or moon. He brought his hand up before his face, and could not even see the outline of his fingers. He shivered in the chill air, and he began to feel cold, lifeless things in the darkness...

No, that was his imagination. There was nothing here except himself and Keldar and Arnul and the other loremasters; this thought calmed him somewhat.

But the darkness was oppressive. The moments – surely they were hours! – passed slowly, and he began to wonder again if this was all that was going to happen. No, there was presently some shuffling of unseen feet, something was happening... were they going to leave him here...? The thought entered his mind again.

But a tiny light appeared, in the far distance, a star in the deep air of the cavern. A glowball on the far wall?

There was some sound beginning too, a quiet, deep rumble, almost quieter than the silence (if such a thing is possible!), half-heard, more in the mind or memory than in the ears.

And a voice began to chant, deeply, resonantly, harmonizing with the silent rumble; the words were from the Song of Origins.

> *Light was not, nor sun nor moon to cast it.*
> *Darkness was not, nor night nor cave to hold it.*
> *Warmth was not, nor sun nor fire to cast it.*
> *Cold was not, not night nor sea to hold it.*
> *Teilyándal' was only.*
> *There was nothing before Him.*
> *There was no before, before Him.*
> *And He said*
> *Let there be a Song.*

And a song *was* beginning, echoing in the cavern, imperceptibly at first, then growing in intensity and volume; the tinkling, trembling sound of a myriad *kitál*s, all playing the same notes but each at its own speed, and the deep slow rhythmic throb of a *túmva* drum and tuned bass gongs. He glanced around trying to locate the musicians, but could see nothing; certainly the sound of the *kitál*s was very near; perhaps the *ahíinor* themselves were playing.

The chant continued.

> *Teilyándal' made the engkéilii,*

and they were the offspring of His thought and word,
They sang to Him the music of eternity.

Voices were joining in the song now, high, ringing voices and deep, infinitely resonant voices, singing a single glorious chord, harmonizing with the kitals, filling the void of the cavern with audible light that seemed to reach from the foundations of the mountains to the heights of the heavens. And they echoed into infinity.

The chant continued.

Teilyándal' made the Four,
and they were the offspring of His thought and word.

The first of the Four that was made is Kullándu.
Kullándu is fire and energy, power and change;
Now a soft flicker of heat in the chill air,
Now the roar of crimson destruction,
Now the burning passion to father anew and forge beauty.
But Kullándu cannot make or unmake by itself,
for Teilyándal' is the Maker.

There was a brilliant flash and suddenly the ceiling and far wall were visible (they were almost unimaginably far away) and now suspended above their heads was a brilliant white fire, burning with glorious intensity, heating their upturned faces; its edges were dancing with rainbows.

Teilyándal' made the Four,
and they were the offspring of His thought and word.

The second of the Four that was made is Tandáalis.
Tandáalis is earth and mountain and stone;
Now the lichen-covered rocks of the sky-touching mountains,
Now the delicate sands of the desert,
Now the fixture of the earth, firm, monolithic, immovable.
But Tandáalis cannot stand by itself,
for Teilyándal' is the Foundation.

The white-hot center of the flame changed to blues and greens, and formed a scene of mountains, high and snow-capped, resplendent in the light of the noonday sun. This was like the Fiery Eye, only a thousand times as enormous.

Teilyándal' made the Four,
and they were the offspring of His thought and word.

The third of the Four that was made is Kewándii.
Kewándii is rain and river and sea;
Now the life-giving diamond-drops on the sand,

Now the flow of the river of water, and blood, and time,
Now the thunder of life and might at the edge of the sea.
But Kewándii cannot live by itself,
for Teilyándal' is the life-giver.

The scene of the mountains vanished, and for a moment the fire hung there, a giant sun in the depths above them; then it spread out and covered the whole ceiling, forming a shimmering veil of light; and then the light turned blue. For a brief instant Rolan thought he was looking at the sky above them, above this cavern, but then the fire *changed* and crashed to the ground in a roar of water, just missing them, and splashed around in waves of a vast underground sea, luminous and sparkling.

One of the *ahíinor* began cheering and clapping (Rolan was sure that it was Eilann) and the others turned and glared at him. The sound of the *kitál*s and voices faltered, then resumed. Rolan's mouth was hanging open in awe, but he almost laughed to himself anyway; this was *ahíinu*, lore power, definitely; lore of a magnitude greater than he had ever seen, and maybe it did deserve some applause!...

A moment of silence except for the *kitál*s and voices, and then the chant continued.

Teilyándal' made the Four,

and they were the offspring of His thought and word.

The last of the Four that was made is Lornáalis.
Lornáalis is air and sky, wind and breath;
Now the gentle cool scent of the breath of evening,
Now the roar of storm winds untamed,
Now the swirling current under the feathered wings of birds.
But Lornáalis cannot fly by itself,
For Teilyándal' is the Wind.

And then Rolan *was* looking at the sky above their heads; somehow the whole ceiling of the cavern had opened up to reveal the blue heavens, and the sun was climbing high in its daily flight.

Teilyándal' made the Four,
and they were the offspring of His thought and word,
From them he forged Tond and all the creatures that dwell within.

The scene remained briefly, then all of it dwindled; the underground sea lost its sparkle and its waves came to rest. It all evaporated into the air and seeped into the rock of the cavern; the sky overhead went dim and then disappeared altogether; once more they were in the room and void of the cavern, and Rolan felt chill again. There was now a slight clash, a barely noticeable (but growing stronger) edge of disquiet, in the music. Was something going wrong with the lore? He glanced around him, but darkness was falling quickly, and the loremasters faded from view. A vague unfocused fear began creeping into the edges of his heart.

The chant began again.

Teilyándal' fashioned men and women,
and they were the offspring of His thought and word.
They dwelt in the realm of Lyarr.
He gave to them aspects of the Four.
From Kullándu He fashioned their hearts,
and their will to create and the ability to do so.
From Tandáalis He fashioned the strength of their bones,
and their faith and knowlege and steadfastness.
From Kewándii He fashioned the Spiral of Life
and the blood in their veins.
From Lornáalis He fashioned the breath of their lungs
and their emotions and imaginations and their longing for heaven.

And then, with pronunciation that rasped in the throat; some sounds had changed into the unpleasant "red" words of Fyorian poetry:

Teilyándal' fashioned men and women,

and they were the offspring of His thought and word.

They dwelt in the realm of Lyarr.

Teilyándal' said to them,

"Do not cross the river Twanéla into Outer Tond.

For there you will find death."

And they did not.

But there was a spirit in the void,

and the spirit said to them,

"Cross the river Twanéla into Outer Tond,

for there you will find endless things to take for your own."

And half of them did.

This was the First Sundering.

We who dwell in Tond are the descendants of those who crossed,

and we have found endless things to take for our own, and we have found death.

We are sundered from those who dwell still beyond the river Twanéla,

They have not found death,

and now they dwell in Taennishland, the City that Moves.

There have been further Sunderings:

The Second Sundering separated languages;

The Third Sundering separated peoples;

and the spirit in the void

has corrupted the Four,

so now Kullándu, fire, burns beyond control or pours from the earth;

now Tandáalis, stone, trembles and is barren of life;

now Kewándii, water, sometimes withholds itself or floods from the rivers;

now Lornáalis, air, brings destruction as it roars on the fell wings of storm.

The music faltered, then stopped altogether. There was again total darkness and silence. So this was the ceremony; Rolan had heard these words before, the Song of Origins was known to all children at a very young age. He had not seen lore like this, though, and he was still trembling.

The voice continued, echoing in the unseen vastness of the cave. There were no more "red" words.

Hope has been given to us. To the Ancients was given the Sword of Law, the most wondrous of mechanas, the power which could judge a man and give punishment or reward according to his intent. For a thousand years the Ancients had the Sword, and they fashioned their own mechanas as well. Their peace was established, and they grew prosperous, their mechanas could hold off the damaging powers of the corrupted Four, and their knowledge and wisdom was renowned throughout Tond. They ruled in peace from the heart of Rohándal, which was then not a desert, but a land called Eyundal, filled with green and beauty. But there was a war, and then the Wrath of Kullándu fell upon the cities.

Thousands perished in the initial blast (which forever afterwards was simply called the Devastation), the ball of fire that roared and consumed and expanded; the few that escaped from Rohándal went into the nearby mountains to die from the wounds in the smoldering flesh or to freeze or starve when the winter came. Now, more than five hundred years later, we have returned to Rohándal, if only to its outer fringes; we have, hesitantly at first, rebuilt our empire, begun once again to wander throughout Tond, collecting lore, spreading peace, and establishing our order; and beauty has returned to the ravaged land.

But the Sword of Law was lost in the Devastation.

Now hear these words, and hear them well:
WE ARE THE GUARDIANS OF TOND.

There are still mechanas left over from before the Devastation, and we know of and use many of them. But others are still to be found; they were scattered during the Devastation, and many perhaps have the powers to bring down the wrath of Kullándu down upon us again. This must be prevented at all costs.

There was a long silence in the darkness. Was the ceremony finished? No, there had been no initiation, no one had addressed him, or addressed Arnul. There had only been an impressive display of lore powers. Was it about to end?

A single small light appeared; not in the unfathomable depths of the cavern, but quite nearby.

It was the Master of Light, standing at the bottom of the rows of benches, holding up a single glowball. The light illuminated his red and blue robe and his walking staff, and gleamed off of the four-pointed star ornament; but Rolan could still see nothing else. The voice began again, and Rolan realized it had been him speaking all along.

We are the guardians of Tond. And it has come to my attention that,
There are two among us, two children really, who wish to join our ranks.

Rolan bit his lip. Now he felt very vulnerable; what he had just seen would now somehow come down upon him. The test was about to begin.

They are very young, perhaps too young, but they have expressed the desire to join our ranks. It must be determined if they really intend to do so.

Another long silence. The Master of Light looked directly at Rolan, as if to bore into him with his eyes. He regarded Arnul in the same manner. Then he turned around, with his back toward them, facing into the depths of the cave. He let his arm fall, and dropped the glowball to his side. With his other hand he let the walking-staff clatter the ground. Rolan had only a second to notice that the four-pointed star had detached from the walking staff and remained suspended in the air like a glowball. But then, for the second time, light poured into the cavern, now from everywhere and nowhere, and now a thousand times again as intense. Rolan cried out and blocked his eyes with his hand, but the light penetrated and he could see the bones in his hand before his closed eyes. He turned away, but the light was coming from that direction too, a searing intensity of whiteness that burned into his very soul. And there was a physical force with that light, an explosion of power that knocked him backwards and sent him reeling into a blinding chasm of the sun.

Behold the Circle of Shining! Behold the only new mechana, forged in the Tower of Kings by Tayon Dar-Táeminos, ahíinor of Ei Eyuhand in West Rohándal. Behold the greatest of our mechanas; the Light that enriches and destroys, the very heart of Kullándu. Tayon Dar-Táeminos himself was destroyed by its power.

The Circle was forged only a short time ago; and its full powers have never been realized.

Now I speak to you, young ahíinor-initiates; Rolan and Arnul Ras-Erkéltis, sons of Tlaen Ras-Erkéltis of Xóa Eyuhand in South Rohándal. I call you forward. Either leave our council and never again be seen here, or come forward into the Light and chance being destroyed. If you choose to leave, you will have no memory of what has transpired here today. If you come forward, and you are not destroyed, you will enter into the world of

*the ahíinor and begin to learn the ways of the guardians
of Tond. The choice is yours.*

Rolan glanced briefly forward again. The light
bored into his eyes like flaming pokers, but he could (in
the half-second that he could look) see that there, in
the flaming center of the whiteness, was the distorted
shadow of the Master of Light, holding aloft,
something... the very heart of blinding power, and it
was indeed shaped like a circle. Then the pain of the
light exploded in his head again and he cried out, feeling
invisible tentacles of shimmering reach out to grab him.
He sat there for... minutes? hours? while the light and
the pain and the terror raced through him; and the
tentacles tightened their flaming grip. He writhed in
agony, and felt the world collapse into a burning cinder
of pure light. He saw, as he screamed, a brief distorted
vision of the other loremasters; they were not
recognizable as humans, the light seemed to have
ignited their skin and they gleamed ghastly white, the
red and blue veins in their faces were exposed to the
air, their eyeballs were transparent so that all he could
see were glowing sockets.

And then another thought came, as if from
elsewhere. Yes, of course it was only the light that was
making them look that way; of course they were still
human, not desiccated ghosts. They were sitting here,
just like he was, and none of them were crying. In fact
they had probably been through all of this before,
themselves, and none of them had been destroyed.

Had he ever even heard of an *ahíinor* initiate being destroyed (killed? burned up?) at the initiation ceremony?

He sat up, deliberately gazed strait forward into the heart of the light. The pain exploded again, but not as severe. He turned away, and he stood up. Shielding his eyes with his hand, which only helped dull the intensity a little, he walked forward, step by step, down the rows of seats, between the loremasters.

And then he turned back. Arnul was still back there, cowering, writhing, screaming. Rolan walked back, up the rows of benches, to his brother, took his hand. Arnul looked up briefly, then collapsed with a sob, his black hair gleaming strangely incandescent in the light. Rolan shook him. He looked up again, their eyes met (Oh those vacant sockets! If only the light would let him see normally for half a second!) and Arnul stood. His legs wobbled and he cried again, but he stood. And he followed Rolan down, step by step, down the rows of benches, into the very center of the brilliance.

They came before the Master of Light, and stood there, terrified but secure that the worst was over. The light continued to pour out its terrible glory, and it buffeted them and tugged against them and tried to push them away, but they stood.

And the light dimmed.

The Master of Light dropped his arms. Slowly the light became the lesser radiance of a sunny day, then of the full moon on an autumn night. Rolan looked at

Arnul and Arnul looked back; they appeared human again, their eyes once again filled their sockets, and their faces were recognizable.

The unearthly radiance was gone. Only the four-pointed star amulet, still suspended in the air in front of them, was glowing, dimly (or it could have been quite bright, Rolan wondered if he could ever call any light bright again).

The Master turned around to face them.

"See the four-pointed star?" he said, and his voice was now that of a man, not the powerful force it had been before. "There are two four-pointed stars here; take them."

Rolan reached up, and took it in his hand. Yes, there were two; one easily separated from the other and he took it down; the other remained in the air. Arnul reached up and pulled it down.

Rolan turned his star amulet over and over in his hand. It was made of a hard, cold metal, silvery and shiny and smooth to the touch, but it was not heavy. Surely it was a *mechana*! The first one he had been permitted to touch, except for the glowballs, and the walking staffs...

"The four-pointed star is the symbol of the *ahíinor*." said the Master of Light. "It stands for the Four, the powers which we tap with our *mechana*s. It stands for the Sword of Law, which we once used to rule a great empire. (See? Doesn't it look a little like a sword?) It also stands for the Sword of Shar, who was slain by Roaghrumtsuk the Karjan, but who foretold of the end of strife in Tond. And it stands for the Four kinds of *ahíinu*, the loremasters' art.

"These four-pointed stars are given to you, to symbolize that you are now apprentice *ahíinor*, Guardians of Tond, and you may begin training. But also they are *mechanas* of a kind, though you probably will not find their use for several years. Maybe you can invoke the Mystery Challenge to find out what they are for!" (There was some scattered laughter.) "But always keep them near you, in your pockets, or on a chain around your neck or your wrist, when you learn *ahíinu*. ...Now turn to face the other *ahíinor*."

As Rolan and Arnul turned around, still holding their metal stars, the Master of Light boomed, once again in his powerful loremaster's voice, "Fyorian *Ahíinor* of Rohándal, may I present to you Rolan Ras-Erkéltis and Arnul Ras-Erkéltis, sons of Tlaen Ras-Erkéltis of Xóa Eyuhand in South Rohándal, two new *ahíinor* in our order."

Cheering erupted in the benches. Rolan noticed briefly that the seat where Eilann had been was empty (that was unbelievably rude!), but the other loremasters were standing up and cheering. From somewhere a drum began pounding, and the cheers grew louder. Keldar stood, holding up the two walking staffs, and then Rolan felt that he should have brought his with him down to the floor of the cavern.

4. THE GROSK

Grask, kachlakksh; tayas Gaejtark-Bad'hanini sh'pfooksh, ash ta'ach tkau greshtaemwopwa 'ahhinor!

"Grosks, I call you forth; yours is the power of Gaejtark-Bad'hani, and you will help to (beneficially) destroy the *ahíinor* vermin!"

(Karjannic, From the Legends of the Magja Tsajuk during the most warlike phase of the Imperium)

In the seven years following the initiation, the brothers Ras-Erkéltis grew in stature and in knowledge. Keldar taught them in the ways of the *ahíinor*. They learned about the lands of Tond. They learned the fighting and fencing skills that may be necessary should they encounter and enemy on the road, since all loremasters were expected to wander to collect tales from farther parts of Tond. They learned the comical conjurer's tricks, and how to set up and use the illusion mechanas of *ii-yam*, the first or easiest type of lore, and about the herbs and healing potions of *ter-yam,* the second. The true mechanas, known as *ren-yam*, third, would remain beyond them until their eighth year of training, except for glowballs; *fyer-yam*, the most perilous of all, was forbidden lest a second Devastation be ignited.

Rolan added to his training his own particular interest and aptitude for languages, translating some of the Ancients' formulaes from archaic Fyorian into meaningful utterances. Arnul's personality ran darker; he delved into the arcane aspects of oaths and hidden meanings and verbal persuasion – despite Rolan's disinterest and Keldar's warnings that such topics could lead to trouble. They both learned quickly, but there was a dark spot in their minds: Arnul remembered Eilann having walked out on their initiation, and mentioned it often to Rolan and Keldar. Rolan would have preferred to forget this incident, at first, but Arnul continued to see it as a grave insult to the both of them, and force it into Rolan's mind until he began to be angered by in himself. Arnul seemed to wish for some kind of later revenge for the rudeness. The opportunity would come sooner that he expected.

Rolan also often thought of the days at the Council Town, but his ruminations had a cheerier theme.

Council Town in South Rohándal; Third Month, Fyorian Year 614

The occasion was Shillayne's Coming of Age party when they next visited the town of South Palms. Rolan walked in to the crowd at the inn (Shillayne's parents were the innkeepers, and they certainly knew a lot of people from all over Tond and had seemingly invited everybody they knew), made his way past the laughing children and the gossiping shopkeepers and gardeners of the town, and went straight for the ten-ball table. Yes, it was still there in its corner, and two children were playing the game. Rolan sat down on the chair next to the table and waited.

Not that he had anybody to play it with; his brother Arnul was a way behind him, with Keldar, and both had gotten quite lost in the crowds. But he needed a little time to think, somewhere where Arnul wouldn't laugh at him. It had been seven years since he had seen Shillayne, and he had been a child then, and so had she... What would he say to her now? Would she even remember him? Would he even recognize *her*? What if he were to tell her that, all during his *ahíinu* training with Keldar, he had often thought of her and the games of ten-ball that he could never win, and wondered if she ever thought of him? What if he were to tell her that he had often thought about how she had traveled to some places outside of Rohándal with her innkeeper father and wondered if she might like to go to some of those places with *him* too?

And so he waited while the children played at the game-table, and he flinched when a hand touched his shoulder.

"Rolan Ras-Erkéltis?"

He turned. It was Shillayne, standing there, smiling. She still had the same blonde hair tied back in a pony-tail (it was slightly darker now), the same freckles and the same cute nose, and her eyes were large and dark brown. She had not inherited her parents' corpulence; she was, in fact, quite shapely (and he was at exactly the age to notice this most intensely). She was wearing a south-Rohandal styled formal robe, sandy colored but reflecting in a number of different but hazy colors.

All he could say was, "uh...Play you a game of ten-ball...?"

She laughed deep and heartily. "So you still remember! Do you think you can win *now*? After all, I've been practicing for seven years."

"Well let's try." he said, angry with himself for not coming up with something wittier to say.

Arnul strode up. Though four years younger, he was now a little taller than Rolan. "I thought you'd find Shillayne!" he said. "Of course that's what this party is about anyway. But knowing you, you'd look all over the town for her if you didn't find her here...!"

"Swallow a whole mango, Arnul. We're playing ten-ball."

"No you're not. You're standing here gaping at each other. *They're* playing ten-ball." He meant the two children; but suddenly one of them laughed in triumph.

"Ten to four! Ten to four! I got you! I win! I win!"

The other boy frowned.

"I'll challenge you to a game." said Arnul, stepping in front of Rolan and Shillayne and addressing the winner.

"What? Oh, sure. You go first," and Arnul grabbed one of the metal balls.

Shillayne laughed again (she'd gotten that laugh from her father) and looked at Rolan. "So that's that. Go for a walk in the garden?"

"...uh, sure." said Rolan, realizing that he's never seen the garden at this inn, and he still felt like a clumsy oaf.

They threaded their way through the crowds, but of course it was impossible because this was Shillayne's party and everybody there knew her and stopped to talk. Shillayne's mother approached.

"So *there* you are. I thought you were going to play ten-ball all day long and miss your own party. Just like something you would do; you're just like your father, he's always playing that game and missing things, and in fact a lot of things are missing *because* he's always playing that game. I wish he'd give away the *game-table* to someone who beats him at it. Anyway this is your coming of age party, and you're supposed to be greeting people and singing and playing your *kitál* and so on; now come with me and act right!"

She grabbed Shillayne by the arm and pulled her away into the chattering throng.

"So that's that." said Rolan to himself. "I guess I'll talk to her later. Her mom didn't even look at me. Well, anyway..." he turned to try to find the table with the food (it was probably over there in the middle of that really crowded place) and he saw Arnul slip between two women and walk right up to him. He rolled his eyes.

"That was quick, spoil-sport. Did you win?" he asked.

"Swallow a whole mango, Rolan. There's someone over there you'd probably like to meet."

Before he could asked who, Arnul grasped his arm and pulled him into the crowd. "Everybody quit grabbing everybody's arm please!" Rolan said, rather quietly so nobody could hear him, and he squeezed through the people with Arnul firmly leading him, and he didn't really try to pull away because he couldn't talk to Shillayne now anyway.

Arnul led him back to the ten-ball table, where, seated on the same chair where he had waited for Shillayne, was a haggard-looking *ahíinor*, his gray hair messy and unkempt. He looked up at Rolan, and Rolan's eyes narrowed. Arnul's constant reminders of rudeness returned to his mind. .

"Eilann Kun-Tanninos. I haven't seen you in five years, much too short," he said. "Did somebody invite you? Must've been Shillayne's mother. One of the other *ahíinor* certainly wouldn't, after you walked out on us at our initiation ceremony."

Eilann's dark eyes were unreadable. "My, you remember well, Rolan. Actually I've been trying to talk to you all those years."

"To do what, ask me why I don't get lost somewhere? We think you were very rude."

Eilann laughed; it was a nervous laugh, but not threatening. "Actually I've been trying to apologize. It was impolite of me, and I'm sorry. I, more than the others, wanted you to become an *ahíinor*. After all, I was a friend of your father."

"Oh?" Rolan asked suspiciously. "So then why did you walk out?"

Eilann sighed. "It was a spectacular initiation ceremony. I've never seen the Master of Light use illusions like that. All the flames in the air and the underground seas and all. It was beautiful. I've never seen *anybody* use an illusion stone so dramatically. But I walked out to make a point. Keldar said he'd seen some things in Borrogg that, quite frankly, unnerved him. So I did some investigating with the Fiery Eye. I saw some things that would make your hair fall out. But when I tried to tell the other *ahíinor*, they laughed. They laughed at me. They called me mad, that the things I was seeing were figments. Such things couldn't possibly exist, they all said. *Fyer-yam* lore had been banned from use; no *ahíinor* are permitted to use it lest we inadvertently bring down the Devastation again.

But somebody's using it, Rolan. Somebody in Borrogg, and it isn't pretty."

"Oh?" Rolan was still eyeing the old *ahíinor* distrustfully, but was starting to get interested in spite of himself. "Continue."

Eilann leaned back in his chair. "The Council called me mad, forbade me talk about such things. And they tried to take away my four-pointed star. But the things I had seen wouldn't go away." He laughed cynically. "The Guardians of Tond. The *ahíinor* are the Guardians of Tond. Quite a title. Who appointed them?"

"Teilyandal'?"

"The Creator? I doubt it. Did they ever say so?"

"Well, no..."

"They appointed themselves. It's quite a responsibility if they could do it. But they haven't even tried. All they do is watch things in the Eye and smite an occasional Karjan warrior with the Circle of Shining. Otherwise they just stand around and look impressive."

Arnul took a step forward, and clenched his fist. "Listen, if you're going to insult the *ahíinor* like that, and after walking out on our ceremony...!"

The older man laughed tensely. "Unfortunately, I mean no insult. But if they would even look at Borrogg; no, I don't mean that... Nobody should look at *that*, I haven't even dared myself after what I saw..." he paused. " Anyway, the Master of Light went and made all that show of illusion, wild and wonderful, but he wouldn't use that power to be a true guardian of Tond..."

"So you walked out in protest. So why didn't you tell me this before?"

"I tried, but the other *ahíinor*, Keldar included, said I was mad, and refused to tell you what I'd said." He ran his fingers through his thin hair. "I don't know, maybe I *am* mad. But after seeing *that*..." He paused, then sat forward and motioned for Rolan and Arnul to bend down to talk to him, and he brought his face right up to their eyes. "Listen, you two. I need to tell someone who will believe me. What I have seen, in these last six or so years... The *gruntagkshk*. Gruntags. Those strange creatures. There are thousands of them now. They live in Borrogg. You saw one in the Eye yourself, Keldar says. But listen to me. They know when we look at them. Only *ahíinor* can know when the Eye is being used to look at them. Even the Master of Light admitted that. But nobody drew the obvious conclusion. *They have mechanas*, Rolan. They have something that was left over from the Ancients. Something they use to know when they are being observed. And maybe they are observing *us*. And listen carefully: they are not creatures that could be living and breeding in any usual way. *They are all different*. Not one looks like another. Some look like nightmare birds, some like rats, some like lizards, some like combinations of all. *And they wear armor*."

"You're not really saying anything new. Keldar's been watching them. But I don't know what he knows about them, besides what you just said."

"He doesn't know much, I can assure you. Deeper in Borrogg there is some kind of... of... tower. I think it's a tower. I couldn't really see it. It's dark. It's very dark, as if no sunlight can touch it. It sprang up in the last two years. Just sprang up, with no signs of anybody building it. But I haven't looked lately. Because the last time I tried, I felt something horrible was looking back. Looking back through the Eye. Something of such malice that it was almost palpable. And *it's* watching us, whether or not the gruntags are." He paused, and took a deep breath. " A thing of such ill would have a name, Rolan. I have dared to give it a name."

"What name?"

He pronounced the name slowly and carefully. "Gaeshug-Tairánda."

Arnul chuckled. "A good story, Eilann. You had *me* scared there for a while. But you know the histories. The monster Gaeshug-Tairánda was created in the Karjan Imperium, in what used to be the Tower of Kings, and was destroyed by the Circle of Shining."

"*Was* it? Maybe *you* forget the histories, Arnul. Gaeshug-Tairánda was *created* with the Circle of Shining too."

Arnul turned to Rolan. "This is nonsense. He just wants to make up an excuse for walking out of your initiation. Well that was seven years ago and he's had plenty of time to think of a story."

Rolan waved him off. "What if you're right?" he asked Eilann.

79

"I'll skip all the niceties. *If* I'm right, if, and it's a big if, the others say; but *if* I'm right, then the coming horror will make the Devastation look like a campfire. ...I don't know. But heed my warnings. Even you, Arnul, even if you don't believe me. Whatever it is, it's in Borrogg. And I think it's much too strong now for anyone to attempt to see it for what it is. So don't try. *Never again try to look at the land of Borrogg with the Fiery Eye.*"

Their conversation was interrupted by a loud cheer from the crowd a few feet away. Shillayne and two of her girlfriends had appeared. Shillayne had her *kitál*, the others were carrying other instruments, and they sat down on the floor in the middle of the crowd. The people formed a ring around them.

"A song! A song!" somebody yelled. *Somebody*? Shillayne's father, Rolan noticed. He turned back to Eilann, but the old *ahíinor* was gone.

Shillayne addressed the crowd. "Thank you all so much for coming. It's been such a pleasure; some of you I haven't seen in several years. These are my friends, Kinnéin and Laréya. Kinnéin plays the *séntem*, Laréya plays the *kétatang*. We're going to play an old Drennic song that I learned while we were up north in the Drennic Lands a couple of years ago, though I'm going to sing it in Fyorian of course. And it's supposed to be sung by a man, though I'll try it in a low voice. Thanks for the request, Daddy."

There was some scattered laughter, then Shillayne began strumming her *kitál* and the others joined in with bell-sounds and click-clacks, and Shillayne sang. Her voice was clear and beautiful, though loud, and people in the front moved back a couple of steps. When she finished, moe applause erupted. Somebody yelled "Sing it again!", someone else shouted "More! More!" (and a third voice yelled "Less! Less!"). There was some more laughter; and another voice yelled "Sing something else!" and then Shillayne's father, as round and jolly as ever, pushed his way into the middle of the crowd and yelled "Food! Food! Chicken in sánatar sauce! Roast rabbit with edible cactus and Shervanya cherry-wine sauce! Stuffed eggplant and peppers with Karjan rice and ground pork and cheese! Spiced sausages! Flatbread with onions topped with cheese and special imported spices from the far corners of Tond! Peaches, pomegranates, mangoes, pineapples! Bread! Wine! Juice and anything else you want to drink! Cake and pineapple pie and Shillayne's favorite, stuffed berry-cake with apples! All for the taking, over there on the table, by the..."

He broke off; the crowd was already shifting. His wife walked up.. "You didn't have to announce it like that! I'm sure they could have found it for themselves! You're going to cause somebody to get trampled! You're always doing things like that! Try to be responsible! And wasn't Shillayne going to sing another..."

Then *she* became quiet. Everyone was ignoring her. Rolan had walked over to talk to Shillayne and her friends, and Arnul had followed. Shillayne's mother let out a disgusted "Harumph," and she stomped away. The innkeeper walked over to the table with the food.

"Well, that was quite a song." Rolan said. "I've never heard anybody sing a Drennic song. The part in the middle with a different tune, it sounded a little like a Fyorian tune that Keldar once taught me. Did you learn it from..."

Arnul interrupted. "They still have the statue!" he yelled, and pointed to a nearby table; on it stood the statue of the Karjan warrior that he had admired before. "I'll play somebody a game of ten-ball for it!"

"Maybe you can convince Daddy to do that. Go try." Shillayne said to him with a wink at Rolan. "He's over there by the food. See? Over there. He's standing right over there. Say, who's that?"

It was Eilann, the old *ahíinor*, standing rather off to the side of the others leaning on his walking-staff, seemingly lost in thought. Rolan felt frightened again. "Oh, I think he was a friend of my father or something like that. I thought maybe you knew him."

Shillayne looked at him. "You sound strange. Are you all right?"

"Uh, yes. Yes, I'm fine. This is a good party; let's go have some food."

And Arnul followed.

The food was delicious, even better than Rolan remembered it from the years before. Rolan and Shillayne and her friends talked and laughed for a good part of the day, before Shillayne's mother approached them and dragged Shillayne (and her friends) away to talk with some of their other friends. Rolan sat down on a chair by one of the empty tables, and then Arnul (who had been silent for most of the conversation and then disappeared to go play ten-ball but had wound up playing *haru-kandis* with another boy) approached and sat down by Rolan.

"So what do you think?" he asked.

"Think about what, you? You keep butting in," answered Rolan.

"No, about Eilann. Do you think he's right?"

"How would I know? *He* thinks he's right, that much I can tell. But as you keep reminding me, why he didn't try to apologize to me, to us, earlier?"

"It *is* rather far to go. Remember his name: the *Kun-* is for the easterners."

"Well of course."

"But think about it, Rolan. What if he's right? And Gaeshug-Tairánda really is still alive. What could happen? Or think about this... what if Eilann really is mad? Or what if he *isn't*, but doesn't want anybody to look at the land of Borrogg with the Eye for some other reason."

"Like what?'

"Well we haven't seen him for several years. Maybe he disappeared. Maybe he went somewhere and found something, say, like a treasure or a hoard of *mechana*s from the Ancients. What if he hid it, Rolan, in Borrogg? Then of course he wouldn't want anybody to look there."

Rolan laughed, then stared at him. "*What* are you saying, Arnul?"

"We could find it. Let the other *ahíinor* know what he did. Call it revenge for walking out on us at our ceremony."

Rolan laughed again, but it was a nervous laugh. "Arnul, of all the preposterous ideas. That we should go all the way to Borrogg to find something that probably doesn't exist..."

Arnul glared at him. "You *know* what I mean, stupid."

Rolan's thoughts were reeling. What if Eilann was right? And how could they do it anyway?

"No," he said. "We can't. The Fiery Eye is a *ren-yam* mechana. We don't know how yet."

"...But we *do* know how to use *ren-yam*. Glowballs are *ren-yam* mechanas."

That was true, thought Rolan. They used glowballs all the time, and he had in fact used one the very first time he had encountered lore-power. But this was just too dangerous a *mechana* to attempt to use, even if they knew which mechana it was that made the Fiery Eye.

"No, Arnul. We can't. What if Eilann's right? Then we'll look at Borrog with the Eye and we might get ourselves killed. No, we can't do it."

"Mechanas can be 'opened' to use their powers. They can also be 'closed'. Quickly."

"No, Arnul." Rolan stood up and began to walk away, but he felt something dreadful. There was a heaviness in the air he hadn't noticed before, and he was sweating. He turned back to Arnul. "*You* do it, if you want," he said.

"The Mystery-Challenge." Arnul mouthed the words.

Rolan almost cried out. His heart thudded in his chest. "Arnul – why did you have to say that...?" Of all the customs of the *ahíinor*, that was the most terrifying. The Mystery-Challenge. *...Either do the deed and sow the seed, or be forever driven mad, by what might have happened if you had...* the old rhyme echoed through his mind. He wanted to say no, but it was too late. The Mystery-Challenge had been invoked, and the powers of the Four were bound to their deeds now. He swore and charged at Arnul in a sudden fury, but it was too late. Arnul had already said it, and they would have to find the answer. Sweating, he grabbed Arnul's hand, and shook it in the manner of the Challenge. "The Mystery-Challenge," he said in a trembling voice.

Arnul smiled back at him. "The boy I was playing *haru-kandis* with," he said. "His name's Ranti. His dad's an *ahíinor*, and they're staying here in this inn. Their room is upstairs and nobody's there now. They have some *mechana*s there."

Keldar was sitting on a stuffed chair, munching contentedly on a plate of flatbread with cheese and onions, when he felt his four-pointed star *mechana* nudge him. He took it out of his pocket, glanced at it; the word "Mystery Challenge" appeared on its metalic surface. He looked around him at the faces in the crowd, saw nothing unusual, and slipped the *mechana* back in his pocket. He took another bite of flatbread. Eilann approached him, looking even more haggard than he had in recent months.

"Hello, Eilann. What brings you to this party?"

"Keldar, I need to tell you something. Now."

"About your usual thoughts about *fyer-yam* lore in Borrogg and so on? You know that a couple of loremasters checked into your ideas, and they found nothing. They didn't see your dark tower. Borrogg is a deserted land, nobody, no *thing*, lives there, except for those gruntags."

"Yes, I know that. But certainly I saw something. And I had to tell somebody. So I came to this party, mostly to apologize to your two stepsons for walking out on their initiations ceremony. But I just told them what I had seen."

Keldar glared at him. "You've been trying to talk to them since you saw Rolan in the Eye that night. I don't know what your fascination is with them. But be careful, Eilann, when telling them tales. They're young. They might believe you."

Eilann seized him and stared deeply at him. "Listen! I think they *did* believe me, and now they're trying to find out if I'm right! I just felt a Mystery Challenge begin!"

Keldar backed off, jerked his arms to knock Eilann's grip loose. "I felt it too. But there are two or three other *ahíinor* here. One of them might have made the

Challenge. ...And please try to keep from attacking me like that."

"But what if it *is* them? Have you taught them any *ren-yam* lore yet?"

"No, of course not. *Ren-yam mechana*s are too dangerous without knowing how to use the four-pointed star correctly."

"Oh no. Listen to me. They might try to use the Eye, Keldar. Dangerous enough if I'm wrong and everything I've seen is a figment. But if I'm right, and they try to look at Borrogg... Does the word '*grosk*' mean anything to you...?"

Keldar paled and backed away as if struck. He scowled at Eilann. "If you're right... no one here is safe..." He paused, then his expression changed. "Eilann, you may be mad, but I'm going to have to believe you on this for now. So where are they?"

"They were sitting over by the ten-ball table. But they aren't there now. Oh, I saw Arnul playing *haru-kandis* with young Ranti Ras-Elrothai a few minutes ago, but I don't see him either. Oh, Shillayne!"

"Yes?" she came over, holding a bowl of berry-cakes with apples.

"Have you seen Rolan and his brother?" asked Eilann.

"Well, I was talking to him with Kinnéin and Laréya, and then Mommy came up and told me to go talk over there. Oh, then I saw both of them go up the stairs about five minutes ago. Why?"

"Are there any other *ahíinor* staying in this inn now?" asked Keldar.

"Yes, there's one and his family in the... is it the third room on the left up the stairs?... Yes, I think that's right. Oh, but he's not here now, he went to the market with his wife and daughter. I think his son stayed here to play some games at the party. They, the *ahíinor* family, are on a journey southward, to the Emb Lands, I believe. Anyway, I think they're staying in the third room on the left."

"Thanks, Shillayne," Keldar said, and he and Eilann both slipped through the crowds and sped up the stairs, holding their *árukand* walking staffs in their hands.

Surprisingly nimble for a couple of old-timers, Shillayne thought, and she wondered what the problem could be. Maybe she should go check on Rolan; he *was* pretty handsome, and he had looked strange when he had seen the old *ahíinor*; but his obnoxious brother might be there too.

"Play you a game of ten-ball!" said Laréya behind her, briefly chasing those thoughts away.

The single shaft of light opened into darkness, and Rolan and Arnul stepped in.

"There's a glowball over there on the table." Said Arnul. He went over, and took the metal ball, put his finger in the hole and the light started. Rolan shut the door, locked it, and followed Arnul over to the table. There were a number of *mechana*s there, mostly crystals and knives.

Arnul picked up a short, stunted-looking knife. "This one," he said. "Ranti said it was the short knife, and besides Keldar has one like this. I've seen him use it."

Rolan stared blankly at him. "So you've been spying some more. And after how scared you were when Keldar caught us in there."

"Well he was going very slowly with the *ahíinu* training."

"Probably to keep us from doing something like this," said Rolan.

Arnul glared at him. "The Eye is only a view, stupid. So what if something looks back. We just 'close' the *mechana*. Nothing can happen. Keldar doesn't trust us with higher-power *mechana*s yet. That's the problem."

"Hmmm…" Rolan was shaking. He waited for a moment, took a deep breath. There might be a *reason* that Keldar didn't trust them with the higher-level *mechana*s. They were about to use the Eye to see something that might be perfectly dreadful, and, and, unlike the *ahíinu* training or the initiation, there was no guarantee that this was safe. But the Challenge had been invoked. He took another deep breath. "So we've gotten this far." He said at last. "If you know how to use that thing, then go ahead."

Arnul turned the knife over and over in his hand. "There's a nonsense word you have to say. Like a spell, except that spells are part of old stories, and this is real. You have to say it once to the *mechana* itself, so it can hear your voice and then act on it the next time. Let's see..." He held the knife up to his mouth, and muttered a strange series of words. Yes, Rolan had heard them before, echoing in Keldar's lore room in Xóa Eyuhand. But that was years ago and almost in another world.

"*Trúmitii káva mikáva ahíkullaa.*"

The knife flashed a green light, then returned to its metal color.

"Ha, it worked." Arnul said.

Rolan commented in spite of his alarm, "Those words must mean something in Old Fyorian. The last word might mean something aboout Kullándu, at least."

"You and your words. Now, shall we do it?"

Now Rolan backed away. The sweat was beading up on his forehead and arms, and he could taste his own fear. Arnul seemed unafraid, as of yet.

Arnul went to the center of the room, and shouted the same nonsense words.

"*Trúmitii káva mikáva ahíkullaa!*"

There was a flash of light, a dreadful flash of light, and Rolan covered his eyes. When he looked again, there was firelight; the center of the room was filled with a blaze that started a foot or so off of the floor. And as they watched, the center of the flame turned different colors and formed a scene of the desert dunes and the sun above.

"Ha! Easy! Nothing to it!" laughed Arnul. "Just like when Keldar does it. It always starts with a scene of the desert near where you are."

Rolan was becoming fascinated despite his dread, and he stepped nearer to the flame. "How do you control it?" he asked.

Arnul was silent for a moment. "Actually, I don't know. Keldar never said, of course." Rolan sighed with a momentary relief. Maybe they wouldn't have to look at Borrogg after all. But the moment he thought it, he felt a twinge of terror; it was too late. The Mystery Challenge had been invoked.

Arnul continued. "Maybe you move it by..., oh look, it's starting to move on its own."

And indeed it was. The scene began to rove, slowly, across the sands. A palm tree appeared, then vanished behind. But Rolan was barely looking; at the same time as Arnul had noticed the first bit of movement, he had felt a peculiar twinge in his side near his pocket. The pocket where he kept the four-pointed star amulet. He took out the object; saw that it was glowing with the same greenish light that the knife had flashed.

"Look." He showed it to Arnul. "That's what these amulets are for; they probably control all *ren-yam* mechanas like this. Remember how Keldar could make the glowballs fly around..?"

Arnul backed away as if hit, laughed, then swore. "I forgot mine. I left it in Xóa Eyuhand," he said.

Rolan almost laughed himself. "Well of all the strange things to happen; *you* start the Eye but *I* have to make it look at..." he trailed off, not wanting to say 'Borrogg'. "Well anyway, let's see how this works."

He turned the amulet over; the scene swayed dizzily in the flame. He held the amulet up; the scene showed the sky. He tilted it forward; the scene began to move more quickly.

He laughed. He was forgetting his fear. "It *is* easy. Look at this!" and he made the scene sway and stagger and then plunge straight into the ground. For a moment all they could see was sand.

"How fast can it go?" asked Arnul.

Rolan tipped the amulet forward, almost on its side. The scene began to race along, flying over the desert like a bird, no, faster than a bird, and the sands blurred into a smear of color. In seconds grass had appeared; they were viewing the lands outside of the desert of Rohándal.

"So where are we looking at?" they both asked together. No reason to wonder; Rolan held the amulet aloft, over his head, and the scene shot into the air and the lands below spread out like a map. They saw the sandy desert surrounded by mountains on three sides, the greenness of the jungles in the south (the Karjan Imperium was there); the endless grasslands of the Shervanya territories in the east. And in the north, there was a wrinkled land of mountains and patches of forest and snow, and an almost circular configuration of mountains surrounding an uninviting brown flat land.

"That is Borrogg," said Arnul. "Shall we go there now?"

Rolan's dread returned. Of course they would have to sometime; the Mystery-Challenge had been invoked. There was no escape. But first it might be fun to take the scene down among the Drennic Lands or Kaii, and see the famous Kayanti stone buildings. Maybe he could take it down slowly, bit by bit, and reveal wonders to himself and to Arnul, a little at a time...

His thought was abruptly cut off. The scene trembled and jerked, and began to tumble to the ground toward the circle of mountains.

"Arnul, close the mechana. Something has taken control of the Eye."

Arnul looked at the scene. "You're going right to Borrogg..."

"Close it! Now!"

But Arnul backed away, shaking his hand, as the knife became hot and began to spark. The greenish light flashed, then a reddish light, and a burning flame burst out of it; he dropped it and it burned and exploded on the ground. The Fiery Eye continued its descent.

They backed away, staring at the Fire with terror-filled eyes. "Go get Keldar." Rolan mouthed.

"No, he'd get angry for us doing this..."

"GO GET HIM! NOW! No. I'll do it." He turned, away from the flame, ran to the bolted door, but Arnul pulled him back.

"Look." Said Arnul.

"Oh no –" The image had fallen to the ground, and they were staring at something dreadfully black. As if no sunlight could touch it; could ever touch it. And as they watched the black thing seemed to rush at them, and open, its left side and its right side changing places disconcertingly, and it became like a gaping mouth. Arnul fell back into the corner of the room and collapsed into a heap; Rolan backed into the table with the *mechana*s.　He reached around a grabbed a *mechana*, a crystal, and held it up before him, and held up the four-pointed star in the other hand.　But he saw, or rather he felt, something laugh at him; and there was malice in the Eye, and he quailed before it.　The *mechana*s fell to the ground.

The Fire exploded into a chaos of sparks and embers that swirled through the air.　The glowball also sputtered and flashed.　In the center of the room formed another black dreadful shape, like a rent in the air, a view into total darkness.

Something leapt out of the darkness.　Something like the incarnation of fear, a gleaming metallic monstrosity.　It remained there in the air for half a second, drooling, rotting, and stinking of venom, and then it lunged directly at Rolan.　He fell back onto the table under its slimy bulk and the table legs gave way and collapsed.　Splinters of wood dug into his back, along with shards of glass and metal from crushed *mechana*s.

The door burst open.　Keldar and Eilann rushed in, swords drawn, flashing in the sparkling light.　(Swords? Rolan had never seen any *ahíinor* use swords!)　Keldar fell upon the creature immediately and began hacking at it with his sword, but it stood and shook him off.　It grabbed at Rolan with its sharp teeth. It had teeth all over it; its very skin was made of molars. It ripped a piece of flesh out of his arm, and he cried out. Keldar was on the creature again, but it turned and charged at Arnul. He squealed in terror. It collapsed on top of him and began to drag him towards the center of the room. Keldar hacked at it again and his sword dug in; its blue blood gurgled out and burned like fire on the floor; Keldar screamed and shook his hand where it had touched. The creature turned around and lunged at Keldar, but Eilann was in its way, hitting at it with his own sword. It yowled.

The thing had a sting in its tail. The tail snapped around, missing Keldar and Eilann (who were both still hacking at it) and it bored into Rolan's side. He felt the pain and the poison rush into his body, and he cried out again. He saw Keldar hack off the tail and dodge another explosion of blue blood; the tail went on coiling and twisting by itself and Keldar kept chopping at it until it was still. At the same time he saw Eilann stab the creature again and again from the front; it kept yowling and it grabbed Arnul off of the ground (Arnul feebly kicked and hit it, to no avail) and then he saw it attack Keldar with its teeth and claws. The pain of the venom was beginning to overtake him, and darkness was falling, but he could see Keldar turn around as it was attacking and stab it directly in its bloated belly and roll out of the way as another jet of blue gore sprayed out; at the same time Eilann jumped on it from behind and began stabbing; it wheeled around and hurled him onto the floor with a ghastly thud. And then Rolan fell, seemingly through the floor, into darkness and confusion and nightmare.

5. RIDDLES AND PLANS

Zn lúmu dáestu zn, íilan ter arn ro estráhas ke hánd ni wártas tóa.

Light and darkness both often lurk where they are not expected.

(Fyorian proverb)

Council Town in South Rohándal; Third Month, Fyorian Year 614

Rolan lay in a fevered nightmare, suspended in a void with endless writhing seas of serpents below him and an unnamable nothingness yawning above him. From time to time some of the serpents broke off from the rest and assailed him, their teeth biting into his flesh like so many knives and needles, and he tried to bat then away with his arms and legs, but there was pain and stiffness in his limbs and he could barely move. A light appeared, shaped like a four-pointed star, shimmering neither in the void nor in the sea of serpents. It was a light which he knew could save him from this horror, and he struggled and tumbled towards it, but it was always just beyond his reach.

The darkness continued. For endless hours the darkness continued, and there were shadows there too, vague unknowable shadows like the creature that had stung him, and other creatures he could not name, and some horrors he could not imagine. The sea of serpents swelled and engulfed him, and he saw that it had no bottom, then it receded and left him hanging in the infinite void.

The darkness continued. Faces from his childhood appeared, twisted and distorted from fear and rage and disease, and they disappeared into the void. He fought against the serpents again. Darknesses welled up from within him and burst out into view, ugly things with no face and no name, and they too disappeared into nothingness. And all around there was that dreadful emptiness. All was dark, all was diseased, all was empty.

The Light appeared again. He was able to turn to it this time.

"What – Who are you?" he croaked through the dryness of his mouth.

There was no audible response, but clearly the light was trying to tell him something. The name "Shar" formed in his mind. He faced it squarely now, and it winked out.

Terror raced through him. The darkness continued.

No, the light was not entirely gone. There was still something there, glowing slightly in the half-reality, suspended before him. It was vague and unfocused, but he found that by looking at it, it would appear a little, just a little, brighter. And now it was again in the shape of the four-pointed star. It had been infinitely remote, wholly other, beyond both the sea of serpents and the void, but now it was very near to him. He reached for it. It swelled, and there was music in it, a sparkling shimmer of sound. The serpents retreated, there was a little luminosity in the void above him. And he understood. He reached for the light again, and it swelled more, and then engulfed him; he heard the sweet music louder than before yet still remote, and then it was gone.

He tumbled in the void again, but now it was not void. He felt comfort, and the sea of serpents was gone.

He sat up and rubbed his eyes. He was on a mattress in a room illuminated by two glowballs, but otherwise undecorated. On a chair next to him sat Keldar. The old loremaster turned and looked at him.

"You are lucky to be alive, Rolan," he said.

Rolan groaned. He felt pus in his throat, and dizziness overwhelmed him, and he lay down again.

There were sharp pains in his arm and shoulder, and horrible aches in his back.

"Don't try to speak, Rolan," Keldar said. "You will need to rest another week before you can talk well. The grosk nearly killed you. It placed some deep venom in you too, perhaps beyond the healing powers of the *ahiinor*; but maybe you can recover from that. At least it isn't doing any evil right now."

"H-h-h-how...l-l-ong...?'

"You've been in a fever for three days."

Rolan swallowed, felt the dryness in his throat. "Ar-r-r-nul..."

Keldar glared at him. "Rolan, there is a reason that you were not taught the *ren-yam* mechanas yet. The Eye is dangerous, it is the power of Kullandu; and it can explode like that. And it turned out that Eilann was at least partly right; there is something evil in Borrogg. Now, because of your carelessness, Eilann is dead. And Arnul is gone, Rolan. I don't know where. He disappeared with the grosk."

Rolan felt the void return. Surely this was part of the nightmare, he would awaken again... Then he cried. Arnul was gone. His brother was gone. And Eilann was certainly dead. And all because he had listened to that Mystery-Challenge! He sobbed, though the pain in his back and lungs was unbearable.

Then he sat up. "Where is Arnul!? We have to find my brother...!" and he collapsed in a fit of agonizing bloody coughs. He sobbed again.

"Easy, easy..." muttered Keldar.

The door swung open. Shillayne walked in, carrying a bowl of water and a cloth. She saw Rolan was awake, smiled at him, and came over to wipe his forehead. "How do you feel?" she asked, though the answer was obvious.

"He's going to be all right." said Keldar. "For now."

"Mommy's made some of the healing wine that you prescribed," Shillayne said.

"Good. Bring it in. He can drink it now that he's awake."

The next week passed like a dark dream for Rolan. During the day he was awake and feeling the unbearable pain, both of his body (though that was gradually lessening) and the anguish that he knew he had caused something unspeakable happen to his brother. During the night he sank back into his fevered dreams of serpents and voids, only to fade into other nightmares of the creature that had attacked him and of Arnul, helpless and defenseless, being dragged away into... into something, and he awoke screaming. But Keldar and Shillayne were always there with him, tending him, and bringing him the healing wine (which began to taste quite good).

There came a time when he felt that he was definitely better, he could sit up without dizziness, and the pains were gone enough for him to stand up and walk around, and he could speak without coughing. One morning, probably the eighth day since he had first awakened, Keldar came in and threw open the curtains, letting in the glorious sunlight, and Shillayne brought in a real meal of chicken and bread and boiled vegetables (Keldar told him to drink the water they had been boiled in too), served with the healing-wine. He ate it, carefully at first, and then with gusto; it was delicious. He sat back and sighed.

"Welcome back." said Shillayne, and hugged him.

It was then that Keldar invited him to come down to the front room of the inn (they were still in the inn owned by Shillayne's parents) and talk with him and another *ahíinor*. It was time for some answers.

He rose carefully, put on his *ahíinor* robe, and headed down the stairs, holding carefully on to the railing lest dizziness return. But he seemed fine for the moment. Keldar and the other *ahíinor* were sitting at one of the tables; there was an empty chair next to Keldar. He pulled it out (feeling a twinge of pain in his arm and shoulder again) and sat down. Their eyes were all on him, and there was nobody else in the room. The other tables were all empty, though there were candles (unlit, it was daytime) on some of them.

Keldar introduced them; the other's name was Hanroy. He was the father of the boy who had told Arnul about the room with the *mechanas* upstairs.

Rolan looked embarrassed. "I need to repay you for the *mechanas* I crushed..."

Honroy stared at him. "*Mechanas* are priceless. They are left over from the Ancients. They cannot be replaced. But you didn't ruin them."

"It was the grosk that ruined them," Keldar began, "The creature that attacked is called a grosk. I believe Rolan has heard me use the word before."

Rolan ran the word through his mind. Grosk. Fyorian *grásku* (the final U was barely sounded). It meant "deformity".

Keldar continued. "It was not a *gruntagkshk*, a gruntag, this much I can be certain. Nobody has ever seen a gruntag up close except in the Fiery Eye, of course, but they don't seem to attack with such ferocity. We've seen them kill things like rabbits and birds, there in Borrogg... Anyway, a grosk is a much more fearsome creature, both because of its attack, and because of what it means. Grosks are associated with the monster Gaeshug-Tairánda. What this means, of course, is that Eilann was probably right, and that monster is still alive, and probably hiding somewhere in Borrogg. Another thing, besides that the grosk obviously knew when it was being observed, is that it was able to jump right through the Eye itself. If Eilann and I hadn't been there to keep it at bay, it could have come down here; and nobody here was armed."

Rolan interrupted. "What happened after I passed out?"

Keldar answered. "It picked up Arnul, I think you saw that. Then it attacked me, but I stabbed it. Then it turned on Eilann; and he didn't have a chance. Everytime he tried to stab it, it held Arnul in the way, so he couldn't. It picked him up in its jaws and it... it..." He paled. "It killed him. I was hitting it from behind, but it was too late. It... it bit him in half. Then it turned on me again, but I couldn't stab it again because it was still holding Arnul. It came down to bite me in the same way, but I managed, just barely, to stab it in the back of the throat as it lunged. It screamed, what a horrible sound, and everyone down here heard it, I'm sure. Then it just disappeared. It imploded, if that makes any sense. It shrunk into a point in less than a second, and then that point disappeared from view. Not even with a Finding Crystal could I find it. It was gone, and it took Arnul with it."

"So where is it now?"

"One would have to assume it's in Borrogg, though we can't be certain. We, the two of us here, tried once more to see it with the Eye, but we found nothing in Borrogg except two gruntags. The land is devoid of life again."

"So why don't we go there ourselves and look around? We can't leave Arnul in its clutches like that...!"

"Of course we can't. Or you can't; it seems like you're the one that has to bear the responsibility for this disaster."

Rolan stood up, rapped his fist on the table. "Now look! I admit I made a mistake! I used the Eye when I didn't know how! And I suffered for it! But so did Arnul! And we don't know what happened to him, or what is still happening to him! And if I don't know how to use the lore and so on, then it seems to me that some help would be what I need...!"

"Of course," said Keldar, "I didn't say that we wouldn't help. But at the moment I don't even know if we can. We can't go into Borrogg; that's a several month's journey from here, and if the monster Gaeshug-Tairánda is there, as we can assume, then we would all die in any attempt to rescue Arnul, assuming we could even find him."

Rolan glared at him. Keldar did not look back; Rolan saw that the old loremaster's face wore an expression not of hopelessness but of absolute terror. He had never looked so frightened.

"Gaeshug-Tairánda is a foe beyond the power of all the *ahíinor* combined," said Hanroy.

Rolan sat down, shaken. "So what can we... what can I do?" he asked.

There was a long silence. Rolan felt the aches in his back begin to return.

"We must discuss what Eilann said," said Keldar at last, "particularly in light of this." From beneath the table he produced a knife, held it up, and let it fall with a clatter on the table top. Rolan almost cried out. The knife was almost like the one that Arnul had used to make the Eye; it was short and almost sawed-off looking, but it was painted bright red.

Hanroy held out his four-pointed star mechana as if to ward off the evil of the knife, and he edged away in his chair.

"This is an evil *mechana*," said Keldar to Rolan. "We thought that all of these were destroyed, but Eilann had one. It is a Blade of Ázugh."

105

Rolan sat forward, looked at it closely with horrid fascination, though he couldn't bring himself to touch it. "Isn't it a blade for making the Fiery Eye?" he asked at last.

"In a way." said Keldar. "The exact meaning of *Ázugh* has been forgotten, though we can assume it was not good because of the 'red' color of the word. Call it a sister *mechana* to the Eye. It does make a flame which shows scenes. But the difference is that the Eye shows you things which are real. It shows you what is happening, as it happens. But this," he held the red knife up in his hand, turned it around in the light, "this shows scenes of what its maker wants you to see. ...That is, not in itself, evil, of course. The illusion stones do that, as at your initiation ceremony. The Master of Light had to plan all the illusions beforehand, all the suspended fires and underground water and music and all that, in detail, and then show it at the ceremony. All of it, except for the Circle of Shining at the end, was done with an illusion stone. And I might add, it was one of the best iluusion-stone shows I've ever seen." He paused, turning the knife around again. "But this, this Blade of Ázugh, was used for a different reason. Just before the Devestation, almost everybody had one or two of these. They made lore-fire that people would sit around and watch. And the maker of the scenes made everybody see the same thing. There came to be many makers of scenes, and they all told stories which were very captivating. In the end nobody cared for other stories any more, only the stories that unfolded in the fire were important. Eventually the makers of the scenes began to control people; probably not intentionally, because they were simply interested in providing fun. But still they began to tell everybody what to see, what to think, even how to think it. Later there was the Devastation, and all of these blades were destroyed, or so we thought."

"But surely the makers of the scenes died then too!" said Rolan.

"Of course. So now these blades act on their own, or others can control them if they have the proper *mechanas*. The four-pointed stars cannot control them," he said to Hanroy. "But something, perhaps the monster Gaeshug-Tairánda, could control this when Eilann was looking at it. Perhaps it was with this, not the Eye, that he saw the dark tower. Whatever happened, I think it was intended that Eilann get someone, preferably someone young and inexperienced, to look at Borrogg with the Eye. And it was not intended by Eilann, or any other *ahíinor*. Something else intended it; something that could act through this knife *mechana*."

"You're saying that Gaeshug-Tairánda intended it." Said Rolan.

Keldar's expression was of deep distress. "Yes, that is what I'm saying."

At this point, Honroy leaned foreward. "I spoke to Eilann. It was the day before the party. The day before he was killed. He was wild that day. His speech was wild. I could barely understand him. He was saying something about, he was going to tell somebody else about what he'd seen. He needed to tell someone young. Someone young would believe him. He knew that somebody like that would be at the party."

"A guess, because of Shillayne's age, or do you think the knife *mechana* told him?" asked Keldar.

"Who knows? Anyway he knew who would be here. But he had something else to say too. But I couldn't really understand him. When he said it, he grabbed my robe and pulled me down to his face. He whispered something like, 'Listen, Honroy. I have just learned something. The Watcher in the Eye does not want me to know. The Watcher in the Eye does not want any of the loremasters of Rohándal to know. But I must tell someone. Listen. Grosks are again walking the world of Tond. There is one man who knows how to tame them. He lives in the Karjan Imperium. He alone is the one to turn to.' But Eilann did not say the name of this man."

"The 'Watcher in the Eye' would be Gaeshug-Tairánda, assumedly," said Keldar, "But a man who lives in the Karjan Imperium? This is news to me."

"Tens of thousands of men live in the Karjan Imperium," said Honroy. "Karjans, mostly. And tens of thousands of women, and children too. Karjans, mostly. So how could we find one person? Or does he mean Shar? Some say he still lives, somewhere in the Imperium."

"Shar doesn't live in the Imperium." Keldar said flatly. "This is probably another story from his Blade of Ázugh. What else did Eilann say?"

"Well, he said something about, let's see... some kind of a riddle. Something like 'In the Imperium, where the sunrise meets the Shervanya Lands, there you will find three helping hands'. He wouldn't say it more plainly. The Watcher in the Eye would kill him if he said it more plainly."

"The Watcher in the Eye did kill him," commented Keldar.

"If he said something about grosks, why didn't you tell anybody before?" asked Rolan.

"You saw him yourself. He was a madman. He was always grabbing people's robes and pulling them down to his face. So I just ignored everything he said. We all ignored everything he said."

Keldar was drawing little marks on the surface of the table with his finger; green, slightly luminous letters appeared. Rolan glanced over at them. They were fairly clear; not Fyorian lettering, but something else, a strange, squiggly kind of glyphs. He had seen it before, little bits of it recorded in some of the old loremasters' thick tomes, proceding vertically down the pages in columns. "Karjanic writing," he stated.

Keldar looked up, as if surprised. "My, you would make a good learner of foreign tongues. I always knew that you sere interested in foreign things. ...Yes, this is Karjanic writing, the Imperial Script, one of a multitude of styles of Karjanic writing. I learned a little of it script when I was younger. It says *Hwatsats Hondrakch*, that is, the 'Tower of the Sun Approaching', which I might call the Tower of Dawn or the Tower of Sunrise. It's the easternmost of the Karjan towers, except for *T'wadzadz*, the ruined Tower of Kings."

"Hmmm. Tower of Sunrise. Is it anywhere near the Shervanya Lands?" asked Honroy.

"Well, no, it's on the south bank of the River Cheihar, near Great Lake Tsenwakh. It's near Ond, actually," Keldar replied. Then he quietly said "smooth out" to Hanroy's four-pointed star, and the green letters on the table grew unclear and then vanished.

Rolan's thoughts were wandering. Sometime, a very long time ago, he had heard something about a

Shervanya *something*, concerning the Imperium. Not Shervanya cherry-wine. Not Shervanya bread, though that was famous. Not Shervanya paper, though that was also famous, made from a grain rather than wood. No, it was something else. No, it wasn't a *thing*, it was a *person*. Definitely. Someone had mentioned to him something about...

He stood up. "Call Shillayne's father in here," he said.

The others looked at him blankly. "Rolan, this is a most unusual request. This is a secret meeting of *ahíinor*..." Kelar said.

"Well it's not secret anymore, with grosks jumping out of the Eye and so on. And I don't think it should stay secret anyway. Get him in here."

"...Well, if you insist." Said Keldar, and he stood up, and went out of the room. Rolan said nothing to Honroy, and waved him off when they tried to speak, until Keldar returned with the plump innkeeper in tow.

"What is this about?" flutstered the fat man. "I have customers to help, and my wife would clobber me if she found me talking to you people at a time like this..."

"Have a seat. You can have mine," said Rolan. "Several years ago you mentioned that you had been to the Imperium. We were playing ten-ball, me and Shillayne and you, and, and... Arnul. You wanted to give away that statue. Arnul asked something about the Karjan warriors drinking blood. You said it was true, or used to be. Then you said it wasn't true anymore. But I don't remember why it was that you said it wasn't true anymore."

"I don't remember the conversation," was the answer. "At least not specifically. But I know the answer anyway. There was some kind of a revolution in the Imperium or something. There is a half-Shervanya *hrakezh* queen ruling now, from one of their towers...Now can I go...?"

Rolan cut him off. "What tower? Have a seat. Now *what* tower?"

"I don't know. There are six towers there, and a *hrakezh* in each one..."

Keldar leaned forward. "Rolan, *he* didn't have to explain that. Her name is Tngp'hl Yathknchul – !"

" – those Karjanic names!" muttered the innkeeper.

Keldar smiled. "Karjanic names... but maybe not all that difficult. It means 'Beautiful Stars, daughter of Shimmering River'. But all Karjans have two names. Her other name is Ai-Leena, which also means 'Beautiful Stars', in Shervanya. That name shows her Shervanya blood. ...She rules in the Tower of Dawn. She's been there for about fifteen years; daughter of Ontárnigraesh and Yathkáani of the royal family of Ond. She banned the blood-drinking."

"Well that's the answer," said Keldar. "Ai-Leena, half-Shervanya, in the Tower of Dawn. The Sunrise meets the Shervanya Lands. At least that's part of the answer. Now what did Eilann mean by 'three helping...'"

"Excuse me, sirs. But I really must get back to my customers," the innkeeper interrupted, and he was bouncing up and down on his feet. "After what has happened several times now when I've been playing ten-ball and all, and twice I've burnt the bread, and several other times somebody's gotten drunk and I haven't been paying attention... I really need to go. Especially if..."

"Yes, you may leave," Keldar said, rolling his eyes. The inkeeper was gone, half-bounding, half rolling, before he heard the word 'leave'. The door slammed behind him.

Keldar laughed. "He's certainly gotten more interested in his customers recently. It looks like his wife has finally gotten to him, though of course that won't change *her* much..."

"She doesn't need to change. She keeps him in line," said Honroy.

Rolan was getting impatient. He sat back down; the innkeeper had never taken his seat anyway. "Only part of the riddle has been answered," he said. "And Keldar just asked what was meant by 'three helping hands'..."

Keldar laughed a little. "Well we can assume he Eilann didn't mean one person with three hands or three half-people or three dismembered hands. Obviously he meant three people, though actually I was never really sure with him..."

"One of them is probably Ai-Leena herself." said Honroy. "Actually I was going that way anyway. Maybe

I should give her a visit. My family and I were going down to the Emb Lands. The Imperium is between. The road goes right by the City of the Tower of Dawn."

"...So you just go and bong on her door-gong...?" asked Keldar.

"Yes. I don't know her personally, of course. But she does keep company with *ahíinor*. An *ahíinor* put her on the throne."

Keldar glared at Hanroy, his eyes abruptly narrowed and his mouth twisted with such ferocity that Rolan winced. "That's a lie. Do you have a Blade of Ázugh too? The *ahíinor* do not care who sits on what throne."

Hanroy glared back, the first expression Rolan had seen on his face since Keldar had shown the blade. "The loremasters *do* care who rules where. If it makes matters easier for us, we care. She banned the raids that the Karjan *tsajuk* warriors had been making. That makes it easier for us. So one of us put her on the throne. It is history. Maybe it is a secret history. But maybe it is time to tell it."

Keldar met his glare. They remained like that, their eyes locked, for nearly a minute. Then Keldar lowered his eyes to the table, and etched another bit of green Karjan lettering (which immediately vanished again; Rolan had no chance to ask what it might have meant). Hanroy continued to stare at him.

At last Keldar spoke. "...Yes... Yes, it is true. One of us did put Ai-Leena on the throne of the Tower of Sunrise. But that history is supposed to be secret; her revolution was not sanctioned by the Master of Light. The *ahíinor* who helped her were renegades, they did not act out of the official policy of the Guardians of Tond."

Hanroy did not lower his eyes. "Official policy is just that. Gaeshug-Tairánda is rising again. We may have to bend official policy. If we don't, we might not be able to guard Tond."

Keldar glanced up again briefly, met Hanroy's stare. Rolan looked between the two tense faces; Keldar was squinting and his forehead deeply wrinkled; Hanroy was staring but there was no aggression in his dark eyes, there was only fear, and a certain pleading. Rolan knew that talk of abandoning the usual customs of the *ahíinor* could mean getting reported to the Master of Light for some kind of dreadful punishment. The stakes were high for such disobedience, with the possibility of unleashing another Devastation...

Keldar looked away again. "You are right," he said at last. "We didn't listen to Eilann because of our official policy, and now things are very much worse than they might have been. So we might have to bend our rules." He paused, then asked, "...So what of Ai-Leena?"

Hanroy's relief was obvious. He answered quickly, "I propose this. I take Rolan with me when we go south. We stop at the City of the Tower of Dawn. We insist to speak to Ai-Leena."

"Hmmm. It sounds both difficult and dangerous. Don't forget we're talking about trying to gain audience with a Karjan queen; the Karjan *hrakezh* royalty are very difficult to speak to, and they are very quick to anger. And the entire Imperium is known for the 'iron fist' of the *hrakezh* and the *tsajuk* warlords. *Travelling* there is probably safe, but trying to speak to someone higher up... Like I said, it sounds dangerous. Is it possible to reach Ai-Leena with the Eye? She does keep company with *ahíinor*..."

"It's not possible. She wouldn't acknowledge anyone in the Eye. She's trying to keep it secret, that she knows any *ahíinor*. I don't even know who her *ahíinor* friends are, if she still has them."

Rolan spoke up. "The Imperium is in the south, and any hope of rescuing Arnul would mean that we would have to go north, to Borrogg. So it sounds stupid even if it were safe. But... We are talking about Ai-Leena because of a riddle that Eilann gave us. And all of this is because Arnul and I, and the rest of you, ignored Eilann before. It seems dangerous to ignore him, less dangerous than going to the Imperium. He was probably right on this also. I don't know who the other two 'helping hands' are, but perhaps we should try to find out." He paused, looked up at Hanroy, and their eyes met. Then he glanced back at Keldar. "I am prepared to follow Hanroy into the Imperium to talk to this Ai-Leena, if it will give me any hope in rescuing my brother from... from that." His speach trailed off; dark memories were returning to his mind. But at the same time he knew that he had to find Arnul at any cost, and whatever dangers lay in the Imperium could not be as bad as grosks.

The two older loremasters were staring at him, their eyes showing a blend of unreadable emotions. There was a long silence. At last Keldar spoke. "You are very brave, Rolan son of Tlaen Ras-Erkéltis." There was pride in his voice. "I was wise to have chosen you to be an apprentice loremaster. But still you are not fully healed, and the grosk put some venom deep within you that I cannot remove, nor do I know what evil it may bring. To go on a journey to now would not be wise. You can't leave with Hanroy, he plans to leave here tomorrow..."

"Then I will leave here tomorrow too. The longer we wait, the worse things are that can happen to Arnul, and maybe to the rest of us. We don't know what's really happening in Borrogg. And if all of this is... is..." he stuttered. A dizziness was beginning to overtake him; and his sight grew wobbly. The ache in his back became a sharp stabbing pain. He stood. Flashing lights appeared in front of his eyes, and then he fell into blackness. He collapsed back into his seat, and slumped onto the table.

"We have to take him back to his room." said Keldar. "We've kept him up too long on the first day. Go get some of the healing wine from Shillayne, and I'll take him back upstairs."

The next day Rolan awoke at noon; there was the memory in his mind of more nightmares of voids and serpents, but now sunlight was streaming in the open window and birds were singing outside. He sat up, trying to reconstruct the previous day in his mind; he could only recall disconnected fragments, like bits of a dream. But he knew that some decision, some dreadful decision had been made, some way to undo the evil that he had brought by the Mystery Challenge...

The door opened, and Shillayne walked in with a tray of food and a curious cloth bag draped over her shoulder. Hanroy followed a second later; Shillayne motioned for him to sit on a chair by the door for a moment. He flopped onto the chair and folded his arms across his chest. Shillayne went over to Rolan.

"Good morning, you're awake," she said to Rolan, ignoring Hanroy's presence. "Actually, I should say good afternoon. Keldar told me that you were going to leave on some kind of journey today." And Rolan remembered. "I brought you something," Shillayne continued, "Mommy cooked this; chicken in sánatar sauce, your favorite. I asked her to make it today; I don't think they'll have it in the Imperium. It is a Fyorian dish, after all. Oh don't look so surprised that I know you're going to the Karjan Imperium; Hanroy is going south with his family and the Imperium is on the way and of course you have to see Ai-Leena to see what you can do about Arnul. I didn't hear the last part of your meeting because mommy asked me to go do some errands; but I can use my mind."

"You were eavesdroppng!" Rolan said.

"Well of course. With grosks and all that, and all of it involving you and I hadn't seen you in seven years... I had to find out a little of what was going on. Don't worry, I won't tell anyone that some *ahíinor* have disobeyed their leader but putting a Karjan queen on the throne... Here, have some of this; it'll make you feel better." She set the tray down beside him. "And here, something I think you should have, at least for now." She opened the bag and pulled out the statue of the Karjan warrior that Arnul had admired. "Give this to Arnul when you find him. Oh don't worry, I didn't steal it from daddy; I just beat him at ten-ball; twice actually. Once was for this. The other time was for, *this*..."

From somewhere she produced a small golden chain which she quickly (and very nimbly) tied around Rolan's wrist before he could even pull away. "Nice, isn't it? Karjan craftwork. The metalsmith made two of them; I've got the other one." She showed him another small chain around her wrist. "To remember this place by; and to remember me by," she said. "And to hope you'll get back safely. Oh I'm talking too fast and talking too much, I'm almost sounding like Mommy..."

Rolan smiled at her. "I have something to tell you." he said.

"What?"

"It's a secret."

She bent down to his ear to hear his secret. He didn't say anything but kissed her on the cheek. She giggled and pulled away, then turned and looked at him with a smile. "I'm not finished yet. You haven't eaten any of the chicken anyway, and mommy cooked it just for you. Now, here, I have something else for you, which I didn't win from daddy. Actually I've got two things for you. The first is mine, but I don't think I'll need it now. I got it when I went to the Imperium several years ago. Actually daddy bought it for me. But now I'll give it to you. Take a look."

She pulled something else out of the bag. An old weathered book, looking like one of Keldar's tomes, although quite a bit smaller and lighter. She handed it to Rolan. He gazed at her for a moment longer, watching the sunlight reflect in her dark eyes, then he turned and looked at the book. It wasn't quite what he had expected (though he realized that he wasn't sure what he really *had* expected), but it certainly would be useful in the Imperium. It was also one of the rare printed books, made with that printing *mechana* that the *ahíinor* of the west were so proud of.

FYORIAN - KARJANIC DICTIONARY

by Kelvas Dar-Túnilaen, Fyorian *ahíinor* of Séyar Eyuhand in West Rolandal, and

Ghrentsuk, Karjan Hutark-scholar of Hwastsats Pfrantukch (Tower of the Rising Moon)

He opened it and selected a page at random.

name: 1.) a name, *hnulka*. pl. *nulka*.

2.) to name something, give something a name, *ksanuhla* (+endings)

3.) to mention something, *nuhraka* (no endings).

4.) My name is _____, *(achhnulkka) ch'*_____.

5.) What is your name? *Ash'hnulka?*

narrow: *shregki* (+endings)

nasty (=harmful, ugly, obscene, or evil): *pargpshki* (parg-p'sh-kee) (+endings).

nation: 1.) country or region, *karchaehnnok*. pl. *garchaehnnok*.

2.) race of people, *ksatsantsekk*. pl.: *gzatsantsekk*.

(root words *karchaehn* [see Karjan], *ksatsahn*, person)

national: *knkarchaennoki* (no endings)

He tried to pronounce a few of the words. "Hmmm," he commented. "The Karjans must need to stand under umbrellas when they talk to each other. ...and what do they mean about 'endings'?"

Shillayne chuckled. "That could be true about the umbrellas. But they say our language is week and unexpressive because it doesn't have enough hard consonant sounds. I guess it all depends what language you speak to begin with. ...The 'endings', I think, are the bits of words they put on the end, to make one word into an entire sentence. In a bigger dictionary there'd be a list of them at the back, but this one's probably too small. We have a bigger one you can look at before you leave, if you'd like. Anyway I have something else for you too. Remember I said that I had two things. Actually it's something to tell you, *Rol-yan*. It's a secret."

"Well, tell me," he said, as his eyebrows shot up at the playfully different, *blue-green*, coloring of his name (changing the sounds for pleasantness, as in Fyorian poetry).

She bent down again to whisper in his ear, but she didn't say anything. She just kissed him.

He laughed and kissed her back.

And then he realised that the chicken dish was probably getting cold.

Hanroy cleared his throat and gesticulated wildly to get their attention. Shillayne laughed again.

"We need to talk about the journey," Hanroy said. "That dictionary is useful. The statue might be a little much to carry. But we're not going on foot. I bought two burros from the stables here in town. I think they will be able to cross the desert if we take enough water for them. The way through the desert is short when going south."

"Wouldn't horses be faster?" asked Rolan.

"No, you can only use horses on the shortest roads in Rohándal. The desert can be very harsh. Actually I've heard that in the Emb Lands they have another animal for the desert. It's called a camel. But here, we'll have to use burros. We can trade them for horses later. Also, we're leaving tomorrow morning, not today. It's too late in the day already. And Keldar convinced me that you're not well enough to leave now. One more night's sleep will be better."

Rolan glared at him. "One more day that we wait here is one more day that Arnul is in the grips of... that."

"Anyway we're leaving early tomorrow morning." Hanroy continued, as if he hadn't heard Rolan. "My business in the Emb Lands is not so important that it can't wait one more day. I'm going to learn some Emb lore from an Emb loremaster named S'Rak. He doesn't know when I'm going to arrive. Anyway I've been studying some maps. We'll head east at first. Hopefully we can make the first *Eyuhand* in two days. It's called Váya Eyuhand. I was there once. They have a famous kind of cactus soup. It's worth trying. From Váya Eyuhand it's another three- or four-day journey to Three Hills. It's one of the biggest towns in Rohándal."

"Why east? I thought we were going south."

"We are. At Three Hills, we can join up with the Great South Road. It goes due south, about three more days across the last desert of Rohándal. Then it continues due south, or nearly so, over the mountains. And then it goes down into the jungles of the Imperium. In about thirty days we'll reach the Karjan border town of Dzokra-Krtsng. It's hard to say at first, Dzo-kra Krrrts-'ng, but the Karjans can say it easily. It means 'Dwellings at the Edge of Wandering'. We can get a boat there, and travel on the River Cheihar. That way it's just two more days to Hwatsats Hondrakch, the Tower of Dawn. Hopefully we can have council with Ai-Leena."

"So it's thirty-two days to the Tower of Dawn."

"Give or take two or three."

Rolan stood up, nearly knocking off the chicken dish (which he had forgotten about). Shillayne caught it, giving him a glare. "If it takes thirty days, we'll have to leave today!" he snapped at Hanroy. Then he smiled at Shillayne. "Thanks for saving that, *Shill-yaine*," he said, using the *blue-green* sound for her name. "Here, I'll have some." He took the chicken dish from her, speared the largest piece with his fork, and bit into it greedily. Shillayne laughed. "Help yourself," he said to her (she did) and to Hanroy. "It's cold anyway."

Hanroy didn't take any. "They have a special dinner planned for us tonight." He said. "They honor the customs of the *ahíinor*. They're having the farewell feast. And Keldar has some gifts for you at the feast too."

Rolan glared at him. "Whose idea was that? I thought you wanted to bend some of the *ahíinor*'s rules anyway, Hanroy. We can eat now and then start off."

"We could, except that, remember, my family is going with me to the Emb lands. They aren't packed yet. I know how you feel, Rolan. But we cannot rush any faster..."

"You *don't* know how I feel. Your brother was not kidnapped by... by something I hardly dare to name. He was my brother, Hanroy. He was also my friend. We have to rescue him."

Hanroy said nothing.

"We have to rescue him." Rolan repeated. "*Now*, Hanroy. I've already waited more than a week to get well, and I might be as well as I'm going to get. Keldar said there was some deeper grosk-venom in me. And the longer we wait..."

Hanroy lowered his eyes. "Very well, Rolan. I'll tell Keldar to bring his gifts up here. And get the burros ready. And I'll get my family to hurry up. Are two hours 'now' enough?"

Rolan smiled, but still kept his glare. "Yes, that will be fine."

Hanroy turned to leave. But before he took a step, Rolan said, "...and Hanroy, make sure that everyone here gets some of the food for the feast. I mean all the guests at the inn."

Hanroy smiled. "Yes. I'll see to it." and he left.

Rolan turned back to Shillayne, and saw a tear in her eye. He hugged her, holding back a tear of his own, and then followed Hanroy out of the room.

6. THE EDGE OF THE IMPERIUM

Tayas dzepalbts Bohrazhulg hragezhnok ash vyorannok, tk tayas rek tsakyats bizhulg rak dzn'raenksh moktsrenk. Al pyacham, tk ta'ach fot tsopfraghtl tremachkrtsng chigtl maha, kyeth ta'ach kotlanwawits kiwarjaennok.

The South Barrier Mountains separate the Imperium from the Fyorian Lands, though these mountains are much less formidable than their counterparts farther north. However, the foreign traveler, crossing them, is still often surprised by the change of the air as he descends into the Karjans' world. (From a Karjanic guide for the traveler)

Mountains between Rohándal and the Imperium; Fifth Month, Fyorian Year 614

"So you've never been outside of Rohándal." said Hanroy as he leaned over the smoky campfire to inspect the wild pheasant roasting on the spit.

"No," answered Rolan. "But I've heard a lot about other places, and I saw a little bit of some things, there in the Eye before the grosk attacked. But this is all new to me." He shivered, huddled in his blanket, and leaned closer to the fire. The air was cold and surprisingly damp, although the stars shown overhead like a myriad beacons in the dark blue midnight. There was no moon, so there was not enough light to illuminate the mountains, but still they were there, dark looming shadows, brooding shapes of deeper night within the night. Somewhere in the distance an animal howled; what kind of animal, he couldn't guess.

Presently Hanroy's wife appeared from out of the gloom and dropped an armful of twigs and bare branches on the fire. She was a slight woman, short and slim, with a round face and darkish hair that pointed to possible partly-Karjan ancestry. She sat down next to Hanroy and wrapped her arms around him. "It's too cold out there getting wood," she said.

"You didn't have to get any now anyway, Andri." said Hanroy. "The fire will last till morning, I think. But thank you. Yes, it is cold. But the pheasant is almost done. Ranti did a good job in catching it. We'll be warmer when we eat, I'm sure."

"I've never had pheasant." said Rolan. "I don't think I've ever seen one, either."

"Well they don't live in Rohándal!" said Hanroy. "Too much sand. At any rate this will be our last hunted meal for this journey. By this time tomorrow we'll be nearing the Imperium."

"I don't really like hunting," said Rolan. "That bird looked so helpless when Ranti caught it. But I think the meat will taste better than this salted preserved stuff we got from Shillayne's town, and this, this, what's it called, anyway?" He took out a piece of the crumbly white bread from his pocket, and bit off a tasteless dry corner.

"It's called *Áyushaa*. It's Shervanya for 'bread for travelling.'"

"Hmmm..." Rolan thought a minute. Funny that he couldn't remember that; the Fyorian word was almost the same. *Árushai. Áru*, to walk, to travel, (as in *árukand*, the loremaster's walking-staff), and *shai*, bread.

Hanroy's son, Ranti, appeared out of the darkness. "The tent poles are falling down," he groaned. "We were playing a game of *háru-kándis* on that board that I won from the innkeeper, and suddenly the tent sagged and fell in on Andreya. Scattered all the pieces." He frowned. "And I was winning, too."

Hanroy laughed. "Fourth time this trip. Those poles are no good. But who wanted to buy them, Ranti?"

The boy shrugged. "Wasn't me," he intoned unconvincingly.

"We all know who it was," said Hanroy. "Now go put them back up again. Tie them up if necessary. Use some rope. There's some in my pack. Don't come to me with your problems. You're getting old enough to deal with them yourself. Oh, and when you rescue your sister from the collapsing tent, tell her that dinner is ready."

"Well it's about time!" said the boy and he vanished into the night again. His voice could still be heard, "I'm starved!"

They ate the pheasant (Rolan thought it tasted a little like chicken, though that was a comment he'd heard before) along with some boiled mountain vegetables that Hanroy and Andri had picked during the day; then Hanroy and his family disappeared into their tent (still rather wobbly) and left Rolan wrapped up in his blankets by the fire.

He huddled his arms closer to his body and shivered in the chill air. He would not be able to sleep anyway, there were always those nightmares, serpents and voids and grosks, lurking within the shadows of his mind. He did most of his sleeping during the day, riding on one of Hanroy's burros, since he was still weak and couldn't walk far.

So he sat there in the flickering light and darkness, and overhead the stars blazed bright. He glanced heavenward. The Hourglass was beginning to peak out from behind the dark shadow of the nearby mountain, its three central stars were gleaming like jewels. There was a fuzzy patch of light below them, he had seen it before and always wondered what it might be.

His mind began to ramble. He had often wondered what *stars* were too; some of the ancient *ahíinor* lore had said that they were like other suns but much farther away; but how far away were they, and how far away was the sun? And that didn't explain what that fuzzy light was. Other old lore had said that they were the campfires of the *engkéilii*, the spirits of light that had been created at the dawn of time; yet if they were campfires, at least some of them should move, not stay in the same place night after night. Well, of course they weren't in *exactly* the same place night after night, they did change with the seasons, but any summer night (like now) would find the Hourglass rising at the same time. And why did they rise and set anyway? And how could one explain shooting stars; neither suns nor campfires could suddenly appear and shoot through the sky...

Oh, there was a shooting star now, there in the north, a glittering spark moving through the heavens. Surely he had seen it out of the corner of his eye, making him think of shooting stars at that instant...

Hmmm; it was a very long shooting star; it did not go out quickly or disappear with a flash of green or red. (It was said that shooting stars fell to earth, but surely if they were far-away suns they would get as bright as the nearby sun before they hit!). This one just stayed there, moving vaguely closer, it seemed, changing neither in brightness nor color. Then abruptly its direction altered, moving back the same way as it had come, though now it was slightly brighter. That was strange. He thought of waking Hanroy to ask what he might think; but Hanroy was snoring quite loudly in the tent (or somebody in there was snoring) so he thought better of it. The star went out the next moment anyway, just after seeming to suddenly change course again and descend rapidly, or maybe it went behind the mountain to his left, he couldn't tell. He decided to ask Hanroy about it tomorrow anyway.

He sighed, fumbled through his pack, sitting there beside him on the ground next to his walking-staff. He pulled out another chunk of *áyushaa* from the pack and bit into it deliberately; maybe he could make the dry pasty stuff taste better by eating enough of it. (Oh well, maybe not. It felt like a sock stuffed in his mouth.) He shoved the rest back into the pack and rummaged around a bit more, pulling out the Karjanic dictionary, and thumbed through the pages, readable by the firelight. Oh, there it was:

star: *kwehlen,* pl. *gwehlen*

No entry for 'shooting star'? Well, Shillayne had said that it wasn't a very complete dictionary.

His mind began to wander again. Hmmm, *that* was interesting, he hadn't noticed it before. Karjanic words were always made plural by changing the first consonant like that. He looked up a word that he knew:

tower: *hwatsats*, pl. *watsats*.

Yes, that was correct. Karjanic changed the *beginning* of a word to make a plural, where Fyorian changed the *end*. But what exactly did the plural mean? Fyorian had several types of plurals. He glanced back up at the sky, wondering if *gwehlen* meant two stars, more than two, a group of stars, or some other meaning.

A silvery light began to show dimly behind the mountain to his right, interrupting his thoughts. The crescent moon was rising.

There was a shuffling sound near him, to his left. He turned and stared; a shadow stood there in the darkness. It hadn't been there before. Some kind of animal; too close to their camp. Two pale pinpricks of light – eyes – were staring back at him. He jumped up to frighten the thing (wondering if this was wise, especially if it were bigger than him) and it didn't move. The eyes seemed to follow him, though. The shuffling noise came again, along with a hiss of breath, and now there was a pungent, sweaty odor in the air. He cried out and pulled his four-pointed star amulet out of his pocket; and used it to send the glowball leaping out of his pack and into the air, gleaming and flashing. The eyes were lidded, and the creature turned and bolted into the bushes. But Rolan stood there, staring after it; certainly it couldn't be what he had seen; a bloblike body with four birdlike legs and a pointed head... a long

132

crossed bird's beak... floppy ears like a long-eared dog... and arms like withered branches sticking out of the sides of the shapeless body. There had been something metallic about it too, various parts of it had gleammed in the glowball's light, particularly the pointed thing on its head...

Hanroy scrambled out of the tent a second later. "What's happening? I thought I heard you yell..."

"Gruntag, I think..." said Rolan. "Something weird, anyway..."

"Gruntag? Here? Are you sure it wasn't a bear?"

"It looked like odd parts, all put together... Look, there's its trail."

Hanroy went over to inspect. "Hmmm. Bird's tracks. Four of them. And dragging a long tail. It goes over there into the bushes. I can't see it after that. Certainly not a bear. That's good, anyway. Bears can be dangerous. Nobody really knows about gruntags."

"It wasn't friendly."

"...And what's a gruntag doing here, so far from Borrogg? Oh, Rolan, look, there's a shooting star."

A small light had appeared in the sky near them, and was rapidly diminishing, into the north.

Rolan stared at Hanroy with his mouth open. "Hanroy, There was another shooting star, a very long one, just before I saw the gruntag..."

"Flyfire. It had to have been a flyfire." Said Hanroy. "One of the ancients' most powerful *mechana*s. It's a crystal that makes a fire like the Eye, except it can fly. Somehow one of those gruntags found one of them.

I've been told they're very dangerous to use too. At any rate, the gruntag probably won't be back. Most flyfire *mechanas* can only be used a small number of times."

But neither of them slept for the remainder of the night; Rolan was too nervous (even if Hanroy's analysis was correct, why would a gruntag, after finding a flyfire *mechana*, decide to come here to these mountains?) and Hanroy, once aroused from a deep sleep, could not easily drift back into the world of dreams. So they stayed up by the fire, talking and drinking an herb tea that Andri had bought just before they had left the town (Hanroy said it was very good, though Rolan thought it tasted a little musty) and Rolan tried a couple of times to make his *áyushaa* bread taste better. Hopeless. No more spooky creatures appeared, though, and Rolan began to wonder if perhaps he had dreamed it himself.

The moon was high in the sky when a rosy light began to appear in the east and almost at once, as if in response to the light, a chorus of birdsong erupted around them. The mountains took on greenish and bluish hues, and now they could be seen as the towering monoliths of tree-studded rock that they were; soon there was the sudden burst of glorious light as the sun itself appeared out of the fog in the distance, and now the mountains were grey and green and brown, magnificent enormous half-alive fingers of rock thrust into the sky, trying to reach the very stars (which were growing dim).

One of the two burros hee-hawed, and Hanroy went over to it, patted it on the nose and gave it a piece of *áyushaa* bread. It hee-hawed again and turned away, then nibbled at some grass at its feet.

Rolan laughed. "I think I might prefer grass to that stuff too."

"You'd be surprised," replied Hanroy. "*Áyushaa* can be delicious when you're on a journey and can't find anything else to eat."

At that moment there was the sound of movement in the tent, and then a spate of curses from one of the two children as the whole tent collapsed into a shapeless mass of fabric and sticks. There were moving lumps under it; one of the lumps crawled out from beneath. It was Andri, who glared at Hanroy. "Tonight we're finding an inn." she said, and helped the other two smaller lumps escape from underneath.

They rolled up the hopeless tent, stuffed it into its sack, put everything else of use back in their packs; Hanroy buried the bones from the pheasant, poured some water on the fire and after it was out scattered the coals and buried them too; they draped their packs over the burros and, with Hanroy leading, proceeded onwards, after Rolan took one last look at the strange prints left by the night visitor. The prints were real, definitely; he had not dreamed it.

The road (if it could really be called a road, it was really just a grassy lane of varying thickness, full of rocks and muddy places) began to slope noticeably downward, and the mountains themselves appeared to become first taller, and then diminish as well. Rolan felt quite well at first and so he walked with the others; and the downward slope made him feel like he wanted to run. This was a pleasant part of the journey, and they told jokes and laughed and watched the scenery unfold. But later Rolan began to feel dizzy again, and his lungs ached; the air was becoming oppressively hot and damp. He took his usual seat on the larger of the two burros and slowly faded into a vague shadowy dream in which the ground was crawling with serpents, and strange fishlike creatures flew overhead, blotting out a weak and sickly sun with their fin/wings. The gruntag from the night before leapt up from out of the rocks underfoot, and then it was the grosk, and it bore down on him in a cold metallic fury. He jerked awake, found that he was perspiring, and it took him several minutes to calm himself.

Hanroy had stopped them, and now the surroundings were utterly different. The gray and brown of the mountains was behind them; the view was nothing but green. Rolan forgot his nightmare. They were looking across a wide expanse of delicate green that sloped away downwards into an endless rolling plain of darker and lighter greens and white wispy clouds; stretching away before them like a vast carpet, disappearing near the horizon into mists. Here and there in the soft expanse were clearings, and from the center of some of the clearings, stone towers, narrow grey and white spikes, stabbed at the sky. Through the center of the wide view threaded a meandering ribbon of blue and gray, a river, and there were innumerable small crafts upon its glistening surface. In the far distance to their left was a flat sheet of dark blue, stretching into the distance to merge with the blue and purple and misty horizon. Five snow-capped mountains thrust upwards as if from its center, white and gray in the morning's glow and shimmer. Near those mountains, black dots hung in the air, tiny and remote; yet Rolan knew that they were probably Floaters, and would be at least the size of small houses if he could get near them. Strange smells wafted by on the slight wind; unidentifiable smells; Rolan later described them later as "spicy, flowery, wild green kinds of smells", and equally strange, unidentifiable sounds reached their ears, much too faint to really be heard, but touching their ears with a sense of presence.

"The Imperium." said Hanroy. "The River Cheihar, mightiest of the rivers of Tond. The Great Lake Tsenwakh. The Five Mountains of Ond. The *hwatsats* towers. This is the view from Mount Shulg. The most glorious view in all of Tond, some say. And the Imperium itself is as beautiful and perilous as any place. The Karjans say *Teshdzart tk ch'hejpfehnnok ch'kajkachnok*; it is your choice whether our lands are paradise or hell."

He sat down on a boulder near the side of the road. "We'll rest here a few minutes. Enjoy the view. Once we're down there, you can't see very far."

Ranti and Andreya took the opportunity of the rest to get out the *háru-kándis* game-board and set up the pieces. This took a long time, and Andreya couldn't find her high-warrior piece; by the time she had found it and they were ready to start playing, Hanroy told them to put it away again because it was time to start down. "We'll have to hurry to make Dzokra-Krtsng by sundown." He said. Ranti frowned at him and Andreya grudgingly picked up the pieces.

Hanroy made a comment to Rolan, "Beware of the air when we start down. You're not completely well. The air in the Imperium is different from the air in Rohándal. We can feel a little of it already. It may make you well. Or it may make you a lot sicker. Now, is everybody ready?" And they proceeded onward.

The road began by going straight down the slope into that green expanse, but soon the hill became steep and the road began to turn back and forth on itself in complicated switchbacks. At the same time Rolan could see that it was noticeably wider; soon they could all ride and walk side by side. There were human and animal footprints in the dirt, footprints covering and obliterating one another; but still they met no one. The grass of the mountains gave way to shrubs and tall leafy plants with red and orange flowers, and soon there were tall trees, decorated with moss and vines and lichens; their branches reached up to meet over their heads and block out the sun. They were entering a dark green realm of omnipresent vegetation and fragrances and sounds of unseen animals and birds high overhead.

The air was still and hot and wet (Rolan could see minute drops of moisture suspended like grains of sand in water). Hanroy was right, that air *did* have a life of its own; it pushed around them and squeezed against them and made them sweat, and it fought against Rolan as he tried to suck it in through his nostrils to get his next breath. ...but it was also laden with thick intoxicating smells, sweet minty smells and spicy floral smells, working to clear his lungs. He coughed; there was no phlegm in his throat for the first time since he had been stung by the grosk. But he was also getting light-headed, and, if he could judge from their staggering steps, so were the others.

"What kind of a place is this?" asked Ranti suddenly. "It's so hot and quiet. Do the Karjans really live here?"

Hanroy answered. "The Karjans do live here, though not here in the trees. We'll meet some soon, certainly. You'll see how they live. Wait a minute..." He motioned for the others to stop. Rolan's burro hee-hawed and stopped as well. "Just as I said it," said Hanroy, "Sooner than I thought! Up ahead, Karjan border guards. Everyone, keep quiet, and do as I do. Generally we should not fear them. Just act friendly. I am told also that they often get bored out here by themselves, so we may be able to get by – once they have decided we aren't dangerous and we've given them enough money – if we sing them a song or tell them a story. I brought some Fyorian silver-pieces. But be careful. The laws in the Imperium are not the laws in Rohándal."

They proceeded. There, on the left side of the road, half hidden in the shadows of three massive gray tree-trunks swirling with vines, were two huts, about as tall as a man and twice that in width, apparently made of mud and grass and vines, and then covered with leaves so that they almost appeared to have grown out of the earth. As Rolan drew nearer he could hear strange half-musical clicking sounds coming from one of them; suddenly the sounds stopped and a man jumped from each hut and stood directly in front of them with hands on sword-handles.

"They're so tall..." was Rolan's first impression. And then he began to see other details. Those faces. Certainly they were human, but they were not like Fyorian faces. The hair, as black as night, and tied up in strange disorderly tufts. The skin, so unnaturally pale, the eyes so wide set; one man had eyes the color of the sea, the other's were apparently reddish, not blood-shot, but his irises were distinctly magenta, crystalline. (Like the eyes of the Karjan statue!) Their noses were flat, their lips thin. Their clothes were loose-fitting and made of several layers; glimpses of something white and metalic shown through netlike layers of cloth and silk, and both wore complicated arrays of metallic necklaces hung with strange amulets and jewels. The man with the red eyes also had a bracelet on each wrist, carved with foliage and the squiggly marks of Karjanic writing. Both wore belts made of segments of interlocking metal, fastened with a bronze buckle like a small shield in size, bearing an inscription in, again, the Karjan Imperial writing. And fastened to the side of each belt was a long scabbard, elaborately carved with leaf patterns; from each scabbard protruded the handle of a sword. They had their many-ringed hands on those handles, and they did not move.

Hanroy went forward to meet them. "*Krichpfangsh*." he intoned, and bowed low, almost to the ground, at the same time thumping his chest with his right fist. He stood, extended his arm, and opened his hand, palm upwards.

"*Krichpfangmosh*." said both Karjans, and they repeated Hanroy's gesture. Then the man with the red eyes stepped forward. "Fyorian?" he asked. "*Ahíinor*?"

Hanroy answered with some halting Karjanic words. The Karjans looked at Rolan and Andri and Ranti and Andreya in turn. Then suddenly they began laughing, and released their sword-handles.

Hanroy turned back to Rolan. "I told them that we were arguing about the best way to Kaii. I said one way. Andri said another. You said another. Ranti and Andreya each said another. So we decided to go to the Emb Lands instead. So here we are."

He turned back to the man with the red eyes, said another few faltering words. The Karjan laughed again, then went back into the hut, came out a second later holding a curious contraption made of bamboo rods tied onto a wooden frame. Rolan wondered what it was for, but the Karjan sat on the ground, put it in his lap and began to thump the bamboo rods with metal sticks, two in each hand, making the musical clicking tones that they had heard a minute earlier. Karjan music. Hanroy was right; they just needed to be entertained. Andreya noticed its deep rhythmic feel, and began do do a little Fyorian dance. The Karjan smiled and continued his repeating, circular melody — no, not exactly repeating, Rolan noticed; it changed a few notes every time around so that after a few repeats it was quite different than it had started. There was something odd about those notes, too; at first he thought that they were out of tune, and he decided that an instrument made of bamboo rods *would* be hard to tune; but then he realized that it had a range of at least two and a half octaves, and both octaves were out of tune in *exactly the same way* so that they matched each other.

The song came to an end, right on the seemingly strongest beat. Andreya tried to stop her dance at the same time but didn't know exactly when that time was, and it caught her with one foot in the air and she tumbled over sideways, laughing. Hanroy and Andri and Ranti laughed and applauded while Rolan tried to get a closer look at the instrument; but the Karjan stood up and quickly replaced it in his hut.

"You... like... my song?" he asked in faltering Fyorian (about as roughly as Hanroy spoke Karjanic, Rolan guessed.) "That... good. I write it... yester... no, last week. I... not name it yet."

"I thought it was good!" blurted out Andreya, picking herself up.

"You dance good... too." said the Karjan. "I like.. end... best."

And they all laughed, including the other Karjan (the one with the blue eyes), who had remained rather aloof the whole time. But then he approached them, and his look was serious.

"So you go to Emb Lands." he said. His Fyorian grammar was somewhat more fluent than the other's, but his accent was less so. "And you have to pass through our Imperium. Then you need to pay us."

Hanroy reached in a pocket of his cloak and pulled out four silver pieces, handed two to each man, then bowed again.

The man with the red eyes smiled, the other made no expression but continued. "You go straight on this road. You travel all day, and by sundown you come to a town. In Karjan language we call it Dzokra Krtsng." (Here was Rolan's first chance to hear a Karjan pronounce a Karjanic name. It sounded quite splendid, with a deep resonance and powerfully rolling R's.) "I can't say meaning in Fyorian language, too difficult. But there you find two inns. Any are good for family. And there you ask direction to go farther south. Great River Cheihar difficult to cross."

"Thank you. *Lachpfangsh.*" said Hanroy, bowing in the same manner as twice before.

"*Lachpfangmosh.*" they both said, and bowed again in the same way. Then they went to the sides of the road and let them pass. Rolan had an idea and suddenly fumbled through his pack (tied to the burro's side) and pulled out the Karjanic dictionary, looked up a word.

"*Lachpfangsh tsrakah.*" he tried to say "Thank you for your song" to the red-eyed Karjan. The man laughed again, but Rolan was not sure if he had understood.

They proceeded down the road between the Karjans and then into the endless vegetation and either sides, and Rolan was amazed at how quickly the two guards and their huts became invisible in the greenery. Maybe the Karjans weren't so fightening after all.

They went straight for another several hours. The road continued in the same direction, and they could see it stretching before them like a gray ribbon through the ever-present (and getting oppressive) vegetation on either side. The air got progressively thicker and damper, until it began to affect their vision; everything seemed to shimmer and grow fuzzy. Their foreheads were sweaty and drips of perspiration ran down, stinging their eyes and making it even harder to see. Rolan tried to alleviate his discomfort by listening to the sounds overhead, listening to all of the sounds as though they were all one vast piece of music; the atmosphere was full of the songs and chattering of birds and animals; singing birds, chirping birds, laughing birds, birds that made crying and chuckling sounds. There was a song like a mourning bird of Rohándal but higher and faster, there was a rough croak of a crow, but lower, and there was the *chipi-chipi-chirrripi-chipi* of some unknown species. And there were other sounds too, strange high trills that lasted until they faded into the distance, and deep calls echoing in the unseen vastness of the forest around them. Rolan could not guess what they were.

After a while the sounds became monotonous and he began to pay attention to the plants instead; huge green canopies high overhead, delicate hanging vines and bearded mosses, red-veined leaves that opened to the shifting sunlight and sparkled with moisture. But those diamond-drops reminded him of his wet discomfort, and once again he felt himself sweating and sticking to his clothes.

And then abruptly the air was cooler and there was a breeze, even a cool breeze, and in a few more steps there was a blast of bright sunlight and the trees were behind them. They had stepped out into a farmland, Rolan saw as his eyes adjusted to the brightness. Stretching around them were rectangular plots of land, each with one or two different types of vegetables growing, and divided from the others by small wooden fences. Trickling creeks ran through and between the fields, and some plots were completely submerged under standing water.

People were working in the fields; tall pale-skinned dark-haired Karjans, wearing wide hats for protection from the sun, busy picking leaves from some of the plants, and in other places turning the soil with heavy plows pulled by oxen and another large-horned type of animal Rolan couldn't name. As Rolan and the others passed, each of the farmers stopped and waved, some smiling and saying a friendly *"Krichpfangsh!"*, obviously welcoming this distraction from their hard work. Rolan smiled and waved back, sometimes answering in Fyorian and sometimes repeating the Karjanic greeting. He also saw the farmed plants as they passed, but most were strange fruit-bearing shrubs and vines that he couldn't name; although he recognized rice plants protruding from the standing water in some of the flooded fields.

The road was still going straight toward the buildings of the town. Such odd buildings, was Rolan's first impression. Made of wood, boards and straight beams, with open walls in some places (he could view in and see that the floors were covered with mats of various types and colors). There was none of the Fyorian adobe, and all of the buildings had perfectly flat square or rectangular sides; larger buildings were simply made larger by adding more rooms, more square or rectangular sections. Some of the wood was painted or carved in patterns that seemed to follow the grains of the wood itself and was probably not meant to represent anything. And then he saw, and wondered why he hadn't noticed it at the very first (probably since he was riding and looking down from a little higher than he would have been if he were walking) – all of the buildings were on wooden stilts, raised a little over a foot off of the ground. It must rain a lot in the

Imperium, he realized; maybe that was why the air was so damp.

They made for the largest building on the left, which Hanroy guesssed was the inn. He was right, and the innkeeper was a Fyorian, round and jolly like Shillayne's father (Rolan realized with a twinge that he really missed Shillayne). He showed them to their rooms (Rolan got a large one all to himself, square and built of right angles in the Karjan manner and with a large bed in the corner, on legs, to keep it off of the mat on the floor, which was green and smelled like freshly cut grass). After they had put down their belongings, the innkeeper showed them that out in the back were two large holes dug in the ground and coated with some kind of hard stone and filled with water. Rolan recognized the purpose of this (although he had never seen a bath quite like this) and immediately dove into one, laughing and splashing about.

"Actually you're supposed to wait until we're gone, and take your clothes off before you dive in." said the innkeeper. "These two are for men, and there are two more over there, behind that fence, for the women. And why are there two for each? I think you've found out, Mr. Ras-Erkéltis; that one is soapy."

7. THE POISON SPREADS

Mordhándu tókaa ra méyeináalis ni, mordhándalan arn Tánd ni árrum, amarn tófyum. Shéi ni, arn fyoránya nol myár hisíyum,"Karjanánya arn anáarislei kághantármas. Keyn anáarislar iyen kágan-múas." Shéi ni, arn Karjanánya nol myár hisíyum, "Eyn fyoránya kághu tármu rénthas káari; imarn anáarislei iyen tamóskas. Keyn anáarislar kághan-múas, raharn tamóskas." Za, khásu no tánein arn nggréshum. Kullándu no ghánt' arn xérandum, zhen mordhándalan arn hákhum, en Tánd arn qaméllum; sya urmáino arn mordhándu géidhalan."

"In the weeks just before the Devastation, mordhs appeared in Tond, but they were hidden. They whispered in the ears of the Fyorians at night, "The Karjans are plotting to kill you. You must kill them first." They whispered into the ears of the Karjans at night, "You have stopped in your plans to kill the Fyorians; now they wish to attack you first. You must kill them before they attack." In this way the seeds of war were sown. The wrath of Kullándu was unleashed, and the mordhs laughed as Tond burned; for they are the bringers of destruction."

(From the annals of the *ahíinor*)

Dzokra Krtsng, the Imperium; Fifth Month, Fyorian Year 614

Humid midnight in Dzokra-Krtsng. The mist settled on the thatched roofs of the Karjan houses, and moved on. From the distant tree-tops came the hooting sounds of the nocturnal birds. A night watchman passed through the streets, pausing momentarily in the marketplace to shoo away a wild cat, and proceeded on.

From out of the night beyond the fog, four shooting stars appeared. They did not fizzle out or vanish into the dark. They penetrated the fog, dimmed into semi-invisibility, and settled on the wet cobbled streets. They remained there for half a second (the night watchman may have seen them, he may not have, but they were by now too dim to catch his attention) and they went out. Where they had been, four impossible creatures now stood. They sniffed the air, paused, and slithered into oblivion, intent on their dark business. The wild cat saw them and bolted, its tail fuzzy, the hair on its back standing up in rough ridges.

The night watchman saw the cat again and chased it away. The creatures slipped by unseen.

They headed with a definite purpose toward the center of the town, slowly slinking into shadows and dim places where no fires were lit. They passed several rows of houses (a little boy looked out; he saw nothing but dim mist within the mist, and gave it no heed) and they came to the inn. Here they stopped. One tried the door; it was locked. They glanced at each other with pale eyes; too many eyes for four beings. The one in the rear came forward, held up a slippery appendage. A pale green light came from it, or something held in it. The bolt on the door too glowed with the pale green light, and then it became like mist and it faded. The door creaked open. The light went out.

They slipped in, through the common room, silently on unseen legs.

"Halt!" said a voice.

A light from the four creatures revealed a tall Karjan in armor, his hand resting on the handle of his scimitar. One of the creatures approached him (he may have seen it, he may not have, he may have seen only the light). From its undefined form came a flash of metal; he cried out briefly (and then his voice went silent) and there was a gruesome cracking, ripping noise, and he collapsed and faded into mist. The light went out. The creature rejoined the others, and they went through the room slowly and padded into the hall.

They came went into a room on the left.

A fear crept into Rolan's sleep, and he awoke, saw a glint of pale light off of the misshapen things in his room. He sat up and grabbed at his four-pointed star amulet, sent the glowball from the corner to the center of the room with its light gleaming brightly.

The boundaries had been shattered between animal and plant, between natural and manufactured. At his left stood something with cows' legs, but it was a big earthenware jug tipped toward him, dripping venom from its uncapped mouth. Behind it was an armored figure, but with bare feathered wings where its arms should have been and tree-stumps for legs (it seemed rooted in the floor) and its head was a thorny mass of spines. There were gleaming, pale green eyes within those thorns. Beside both, mounted on a rat the size of a large pig, was something carved from a dead tree but sporting a scaly lizard's tail and a sickly six-eyed human-ish face leering from a crack in the wood. To the right was a green-skinned (and apparently rotting) thing like a man, its eyes completely round and protruding from their sockets, its mouth a reptilian beak, its bald head scaly and shining luridly in the light, its gnarled, long-fingered claw resting on a Karjan-style sword strapped to its waist.

They all stood there, unmoving, unblinking, staring at Rolan.

He was too afraid to move. Surely they were here to kill him, to finish what the grosk had begun... The grosk... In his mind's eye he saw its scaly bulk collapse on him, and he cried out in terror and rage. And that terror and rage became like a physical thing, a living being that he could fight, and he transferred it to these horrid things here in his room. A hideous yowl escaped from his mouth and he grabbed his walking-staff, knocked the end off to expose the sword, and attacked them, flailing and slashing blindly, and a pale metallic light gleamed from his hands and eyes. The creatures dodged his blows and faded into mist and were gone, leaving him shaking and crying on the floor.

The light was still in his eyes and coming out of his hands when Hanroy came in, sword in hand, but it vanished immediately.

"What happened?" asked Hanroy.

"Gruntags. Four of them." Rolan stuttered. "They came in here. They just stood there, and..."

"Rolan! Your hand!"

Rolan looked at his hand, where the strange light had been shining. There was a scaly green patch there, on the back of that hand, and it shown obscenely in the light of the glowball. Rolan backed away, toward the bed, and collapsed with a sob, dropping his sword. Hanroy went over and hugged him. Out of the window, they both briefly saw four shooting stars, traveling as a group, leap into the air from somewhere near the inn.

A scream rent the air. And another scream, almost like an animal's yowl. Then a chill silence.

"They're still here!" blurted Hanroy. "Somebody else saw them too! It came from out in the hall... Rolan, get your sword."

Rolan was still staring at the ugly patch on the back of his hand, his eyes wide.

Hanroy slapped him. "I don't know what that is. But look at it later! Somebody might be being killed!"

Slowly Rolan stood, and faced Hanroy as another scream echoed through the building. "All right," he said at last. He took his sword from where he had dropped it, and followed Hanroy out into the hall.

There were already some other people awake and running toward the source of the screams. Rolan recognized the innkeeper among them, and several Karjans that he had seen the day before. Andri was standing by the door to Hanroy's room.

"What's happening?" she asked.

"Don't know. Stay here!" said Hanroy. Then he turned to everyone else. "Everybody stay here! Except you, innkeeper. But keep behind me. Rolan, come here."

Rolan followed. The three of them ran out into the large center room, and they could see nothing amiss. There was a fire lit in the large fireplace, lighting the dark scene. There was an open book on one of the tables, and a half-full goblet of water.

"Everything's in order, except all this mist." said the innkeeper. "What is all of this mist, anyway!? And where is Arghak?" (He meant the watchman.)

One more scream, very near, there in the room. It was a pitiful yowl, fading into agonized silence.

The innkeeper turned to Rolan and Hanroy, his eyes suddenly wide. "There were words in that last scream. Karjanic words. But I couldn't understand them..."

Rolan grabbed Hanroy's shoulder. "... He's right. I heard words too. But, it was coming from there, right in the middle of the mist..."

"There's nothing there!" exclaimed the innkeeper.

Hanroy's eyebrows went up. "There is *too* something there! You two stay here! I'll go get my pack from Andri..."

He turned, only to bump into Andri, who was holding his pack. "I thought I told you to stay in the room!" he blurted, then, "...Thank you for the pack. I need a *mechana*..."

"...I did stay back to make sure the children were asleep," said Andri.

Hanroy threw his pack on the ground and rummaged through it while the innkeeper replied to the scream with words of his own, in Karjanic. There was no reply.

Hanroy pulled something out of his pack, put it in his pocket. He pulled out something else. "Here. Rolan, hold this crystal. When I say so, throw it into the center of the mist. But not before I say so."

He went in front of the others, he sword ready, and stood before the place where the screams had come from. "Where are you?" he yelled into the mist. Silence. "Can you here me?" he yelled again. There came a quiet whimper from the center of the mist. As if that was a cue, he pulled the thing from his pocket and dropped it on the floor, crushing it with his foot. A green light flooded the room, and their vision was transformed. The walls and the floor and the table faded into near imperceptibility, the fire was now black, but the air itself had become like a pale green gas that gathered and swirled around itself; the currents and eddies of the wind were visible. And other things had appeared too, formless patterns of light and shade, and tiny points of light like stars but much closer and there in the room. And in in front of Hanroy, where the screams had come from, there lay an armored Karjan warrior on the floor, his curved scimitar fallen at his side, his face an apparition of pure terror, his chest ripped apart into a huge gaping, ragged wound. He turned and faced them, his body flexed and contorted briefly, and then he was still.

"It's Arghak!" explaimed the innkeeper.

"Now, Rolan, the crystal," said Hanroy.

Rolan threw the crystal. It seemed to travel slowly through the visible air, spinning and tumbling. It hit the floor and there was a flash of white light.

That was all. The green light was gone. The room took on its normal hues. The Karjan was visible too, and around him was a pile of dust. Hanroy ran over to him, knelt down beside him.

"He's dead. Somebody killed him with a flaysword. They missed his heart and his lungs at least. Then they used a *mechana* so we couldn't find him. Until it was too late. Not that anybody can usually survive a flaysword anyway..."

Hours later, when the sun was beginning to rise, Hanroy follwed Rolan into Rolan's room, and his face was grim. "Eilann was right about this too," he said. "The gruntags have *mechana*s. They used a hiding crystal on Arghak. They caught him unaware, I think. His book and his glass were still there on the table." Then, responding to Rolan's questioning expression, "What a hiding crystal does is scatter light. You can only see things because light bounces off of them. A hiding crystal makes a fine dust. It bounces light in all directions. And it surrounds things. So whatever it surrounds becomes nearly invisible. And if you're surrounded, you can't see well either. Anyway I used a finding crystal to find him. And to make sure that he wasn't something else, like a gruntag. A finding crystal gives off a strange light that usually you can't see. It makes invisible things visible. You can see the air. And those little lights like stars, those are animals far too small to see. There are millions of them everywhere. Anyway, then you used an unhiding crystal to dispel the dust and make it fall to the floor. So he became visible again. Hiding and unhiding crystals are always used together. Except that the gruntags probably meant to leave him like that. So nobody could find him. Or find his body. Until they tripped over him. Anyway, I don't have any more of those crystals."

He sat down on the chair next to Rolan's bed. "And that explains how the gruntags got in here too. They had a hiding crystal on themselves. I don't know how they could see. Maybe they don't need to see.

Anyway I think Arghak saw them, or part of them. He tried to stop them. So they killed him. Probably used something else to put him asleep at first too. He didn't start screaming until after they were gone from here. Or maybe they put the crystal on him later. Anyway we still don't know why they came. Let me have a look at that hand, Rolan."

Rolan showed him his infected hand. The skin had peeled away from the green patch, which seemingly had grown from within, and it stuck out slightly and was toothy and metallic.

Hanroy swore. "This is all beginning to make sense." He said grimly. "And it's worse than I had thought. Worse than Eilann had thought. Though I don't really know how much he knew. Anyway we have to get to Ai-Leena as soon as possible. Before you become dangerous yourself. Get your pack ready now. We'll have to leave for Hwatsats Hondrakch immediately."

Rolan stared at him. "What is it? What is happening...?"

Hanroy only replied, "I don't think I could tell you all. Anyway you want to try to rescue Arnul. Get your pack ready or there won't be any time." And he went out the door.

Misty dawn in Dzokra-Krtsng. The air was already hot and heavy, and the red light of sunrise stabbed through the clouds. There were a few people about; going about their business of setting up the market or going out to the fields to work; none had any idea of the horrors that had occurred in the inn the night before. Hanroy apologized to the innkeeper for not helping with the funeral preparations for Arghak, since he had seen him die, but he gave him an extra several day's worth of pay for their room, and then he led Rolan and the others on their burros out of the town.

Rolan was beginning to feel sick, and he rode sullenly. The horror was still fresh in his mind, the misshapen monsters, the patch on his hand, the screams and the gaping bloody wound in Arghak's chest. Like the wound had been caused from the inside, from something exploding outward. Hanroy had mentioned a flaysword; Rolan had heard rumors of that horrible weapon, of fiendish Karjanic design; a single blade went in, one pulled the handle, and the blade opened into four, and one pulled it out. The gruntags had such a weapon, and they had *mechana*s. And they were trying to attack him, or, it seemed, get him to attack them. At the thought of that, there seemed to be a dark fury welling up deep within his mind, wanting to break out and cause destruction. He swallowed hard and tried to ignore it. He looked at the green patch on his hand; it was darker now, almost black, but it had not grown or changed shape.

There was a peal of thunder overhead and the rain began. Pouring down on Rolan's face, it refreshed him somewhat and chased away his darker fears. A moment later they stepped into the thick vegetation at the side of the town, and were once again plodding through the seamless jungles of the Imperium. The road went along strait again for a few minutes, then made a sharp turn to the left and began to descend rapidly. The vegetation opened up again after a few more minutes, and they were standing at the edge of a river.

And what a river. The surface was dark blue and black, and flowing silently with a hint of unimaginable power. Rolan strained to see the far side through the mist and rain; it looked as if it was a mile or more away.

The road split into two directions, and they went left. Almost immediately there came the sounds of talking and of people and the splash of waves, and some other musical thumpings. The mist was thicker so Rolan didn't see at first that they had stepped out onto a wooden platform (though he could hear the buro's feet clattering on it).

The rain cleared suddenly. They were standing on a platform from which jutted many piers out into the river; tied to some of the piers were open boats, made of wood and decorated with carvings of sea monsters. There were Karjans in all of them, some sitting by the oars, others merely stretched out, relaxing. They didn't seem to mind the rain. Four men in one of the boats were playing on musical instruments; one on a set of bamboo rods like Rolan had seen before, one on a similar instrument made of wood, one on an upright stringed instrument (that would be a harp) and one on a *kital*. Their music was of the same type as that of the border guards, if somewhat fuller because of the four instruments; a rhythmic music, out of tune in such a way that it was actually in tune (even the *kital* was tuned like that!), and, Rolan realized, the four parts didn't actually match. They were merely in the same rhythm, and stopped and started at the same time. As if trying to be the opposite of Fyorian music, where the parts always matched harmonically but were not necessarily on the beat.

Hanroy went over to the nearest large boat. The man at the front jumped up and then bowed, the same way as Rolan had seen. He was dressed in loose-fitting white and grey robes, tied about the waist with a rope and an enormous buckle. Hanroy repeated the bow.

"Boat to Hwatsats Hondrakch. How much? Less if I trade burros?" asked Hanroy in simple Fyorian.

"I'll take your burros, but we can't go now." the Karjan replied, fluently in the same language. "There's a boat from there coming here; we see it over there on the river. It's a royal boat; we have to be here to greet the *hrakezh* lords when they get off."

Rolan gazed across the river to where he had pointed. There was a boat there, painted bright red, approaching from upstream.

Hanroy turned back to Rolan. "Well, of all the luck. They had to come now. We need to hurry... Wait." Then he wheeled back around to the boatman. "*Where* did you say they were from?"

"Can't be certain, but it's a royal boat, painted red, you know, and there's only one place upstream there where a royal boat would be likely to come from. That's

Hwatsats Hondrakch, the Tower of Dawn. The place you said you wanted to go to anyway."

"And indeed I did!" said Hanroy, almost laughing. "We were going there to see the *hrakezh*. But if they're coming here... They might not stop here, though. *Why* are they coming?"

The boatman replied, "If I knew that, I could make a fortune in reading peoples' minds, you know."

Hanroy turned back to Rolan. "So there's nothing to do but wait." he said, and sat down on the wood.

"Play you a game of *háru-kándis*!" said Ranti to Andreya, and rummaged through his small pack. "What is, eww, moldy." He pulled out a fuzzy piece of *áyushaa* bread and threw it in the river.

"It goes bad quickly in the wet Karjan air," commented Hanroy.

"It was bad to begin with," said Rolan.

They waited while the red boat approached. Rolan watched it closely; it was much larger than the boats here in the harbor and it had a covered cabin in the center. There were several Karjans riding on it, five tall men with their dark hair tied up in those strange stiff tufts, and five tall women, with longer dark hair pulled back in pony-tails and held in place with golden rings; all were dressed in the loose-fitting Karjan robes (but much more colorful than Rolan had seen before), and most were wearing large bracelets and chain necklaces. And they were all carrying curved Karjan swords. At the front of the boat, painted in white on the red background, were two large square characters of some kind of squiggly writing, different from the Karjanic scripts Rolan had already seen.

At a command from someone on the boat, the riders sat down and put oars out into the water (Rolan suddenly realized that he hadn't seen anything to move the boat...!) and the boat turned and began to head for the piers. There was a rush of water as it docked, and one of the men at the front produced a thick rope and tied it up. Hanroy bowed in the Karjan manner as the people stepped off, and everyone else there at the pier bowed too, except for the four musicians, who began to play a slower and more solemn tune (or *four* slower and more solemn tunes; Rolan was still not sure if the parts actually fit together.)

The Karjans from the boat formed two lines on the pier, the men on one side and the women on the other, and they raised their swords in a salute. The man closest to the boat proclaimed some consonant-rich words in Karjaneic ("*Pfreshtakj Hwatsats Hondrakchchi 'rakezh!*") and then, apparently noticing Rolan and the others among them, in Fyorian. "Make way for the *hrakezh* lords of the Tower of Dawn!" And then all were silent.

The door in the cabin in the middle of the boat opened and three men stepped out. Not Karjans, to Rolan's surprise. The first was a large man, as tall as the Karjans but much broader, with brown skin darker than that of a Fyorian; his wavy black hair combed neatly and lacking in any kind of adornment. He wore a Karjan robe, but not as elaborate as the others, and a wooden amulet dangling from a string around his neck was carved into rounded, flattened characters that appeared to be yet another style of Karjan writing. The second man was of very curious appearance, wearing a bright green robe that appeared to be made of leaves but there were no seams visible in it. He wore no jewelry or adornments. His skin was about the same color as that of a Fyorian, his face was youthful, without lines or wrinkles, but there was the look of great age and wisdom in his eyes. Those eyes were... some other color. Rolan was sure that it *was* a color, but it was not a color that he had seen before, anywhere. There were no words in his mind for that color.

The third man was a Fyorian, bearded, a little older than Hanroy, and dressed in the heavy flowing robe of a high-ranking *ahíinor*. As if to complete the appearance, he carried a crooked *árukand* walking-staff, topped with a four-pointed star, although he also had a sword strapped to his waist, Karjan-style; yet its silver handle was plain and undecorated. His nose was long, like many a Fyorian, and he was shorter than anyone there, and his bare arms were quite muscular. He regarded the scene with thoughtful (and, Rolan thought, somewhat fearful) dark brown eyes, and then he spotted Hanroy, and bowed in the Fyorian manner.

Hanroy bowed back like an *ahíinor*. Rolan tried to do the same bow, and nearly fell off the burro. There was some scattered laughter, suddenly cut short. The man with the green robe and the strange eyes had seen Rolan, and then his face changed to an expression that

Rolan had never seen: horror, perhaps, or a sadness that could not be fathomed. He said something in Karjanic to the Fyorian.

The Fyorian turned and looked at Rolan, and his eyes narrowed. He turned back to the others, barked an order in Karjanic, and they went back on the boat.

"What's... what's happening...?" asked Rolan.

The *ahíinor* from the boat turned back to Rolan and the others. "I'm sorry for being rude." He said. "Things are happening too fast. Allow me to introduce ourselves. This is S'Tam, son of S'Tai, Lord of Arsh in the Emb Lands. He is a visitor to Hwatsats Hondrakch, but he asked if he could come along on the boat trip." The dark man bowed again. "...And this is Nammar the Taennishman." The man in the green robe also bowed again. "And my name is Tayon Dar-Táeminos, *ahíinor* of West Rohándal, presently serving as underlord to *Hrakezh Tngp'hl Yathknchul* Queen Ai-Leena of Hwatsats Hondrakch."

He went on the introduce each of the Karjans in the boat, who took a moment to stand up and bow as they were getting the oars ready. But Rolan was no longer listening. *Taennishman*? One of the Immortals, those who dwelt in Taennishland, the City that Moves? And Tayon Dar-Táeminos? *The* Tayon Dar-Táeminos, who had forged the Circle of Shining in the ruined Tower of Kings? It was as if legends had suddenly sprung up out of the river. No, that couldn't *all* be correct, though; the legend clearly said that the Tayon Dar-Táeminos who had forged the Circle of Shining had been destroyed by its power, so this had to be another man by the same name. There were many Fyorians named Tayon; and Táeminos was a fairly common surname as well, with or without the *Dar-* for the Fyorians of the West.

He was explaining something when Rolan's attention returned to the present situation. "...So when we saw the flyfires land in Dzokra-Krtsng last night, we got the boat ready and came. We had seen some on the mountains the night before, and a few in the sky, northwards, before that. Nammar was afraid that they might be gruntags."

"They *were* gruntags." Hanroy answered. "They attacked us. They killed a man in the inn. With a flaysword. And they put a hiding crystal on him. Then they went to Rolan's room. Show him your hand, Rolan."

Rolan held up the hand with the dark green patch. Tayon looked at it gravely, and the Taennishman inspected it too. "Dog feathers! This is worse than we feared," said Tayon at last. "The gruntags came with a reason. And they will come again tonight, or I'm a Karjan. He may not..." His speech trailed off. He turned to the others, barked another order. Two of the men got off and ran off of the pier down the road into the forest.

"All of you get on the boat, including your burros and all your belongings," he said to Rolan and Hanroy. "We'll put you up in Hwatsats Handrak for free. It'll take until tomorrow evening to get there, and that may be too late if they attack again."

"Until tomorrow night?" said Hanroy. "You said you came when you saw the flyfires. It took you only a couple of hours."

"Seven hours, yes, going downstream. Going upstream is more difficult, and we'll have to row. Get on the boat. You must see all Ai-Leena immediately. Sooner than immediately."

Tayon paid each of the boatmen a large silver coin (for not being able to get paid by these travellers, he said), and Rolan and the others got on the boat. Rolan went first; he had never been on a boat before, and he nearly slipped on its wooden floor. One of the Karjan women grabbed him to keep him from falling over; he smiled at her and sat down on the bench next to her. Andri followed Rolan, and sat behind him; Ranti and Andreya behind her, and Hanroy in the rear, then the Taennishman and the Emb, and finally Tayon. At Tayon's order the other Karjans held the oars and pushed the boat off from the pier onto the waters of the Great River Cheihar. The two men who had run down the road into town did not return. They had left to make room, Rolan figured, since the boat was now crowded as it was.

This part of the journey was the most monotonous for Rolan, once he got over the novelty of the boat and the new companions. Everyone was silent, and the air was hot and heavy and began to reek with sweat from all the Karjans (and Tayon and Nammar and Hanroy) rowing. The oars slipped in the water and out again endlessly, beating out a dull changeless rhythm. The burros stood sullenly in the back of the boat. The river passed underneath of them with sickening sameness, grey and greenish (and sometimes black) and on both sides there was simply more and more thick vegetation. The sky clouded over again and it began to drizzle a hot, steamy rain that ran down Rolan's hair and into his eyes, stinging like salt. He began to fall into an uncomfortable dream, again with ugly creatures flying overhead on what could be either fins or wings. Then there were hideous things standing all around, staring at him; vague shadows that writhed and boiled, things that were part man and part animal. And the grosk was there in the middle of them, and its tail whipped around and tried to sting him; he jumped up with a start.

The dream was over, but he was feeling feverish and chilled; the rain was soaking his clothes. The others were staring at him, their lips tight in grim expressions. The Taenishman stood up in the back and stretched his arms out said something gently in a strange language that was more musical than linguistic; the rains parted and the sunshine stabbed through.

"Never underestimate the Taennish power," said Tayon.

"There is no Taennish power," replied the Taennishman.

Tayon shrugged.

One of the Karjans released his oars and went into the cabin for a moment, returning with a tray of slices of bread and fruit. "Lunch time," he said. They all helped themselves; to Rolan the fruit was delicious and it helped clear his mind and he felt a little better. He recognized mango and pineapple; some of the others were strange but tasty. He realized that he hadn't actually tried any Karjan food yet, either (the Fyorian innkeeper had served a Fyorian dinner of chicken and edible cactus).

The sun was beginning to set, almost directly behind them, when at last Rolan dared to ask the question. "What is it?" he asked. "What is happening? Why all this hurry...?"

"You wanted to rescue Arnul." Said Hanroy. The others were silent.

"There is something besides that."

It was the Taennishman who answered, and his voice was ever-so-gentle and calming. "My dear sir, do you really need to know what would cause you to despair? You are safe here with us; that is all you need to know for the time being."

Rolan stood, and faced the Taennishman with narrow eyes. "Maybe that's all I *need* to know, but I would *like* to know something else!" he yelled. "You're all rowing, for much longer than I thought it was possible for anyone to row, and you're trying to get me to see Ai-Leena as soon as possible! Well this much I wanted to do anyway; Eilann said that if there was any hope to rescue my brother I had to see Ai-Leena! But something else is happening now! I know it is dreadful, but why can't anyone tell me!? I think I deserve to know the answers!"

He paused, looked at the grim faces around him, and back to the Taennishman. To his surprise, Nammar was weeping. Tears stained his cheeks. "Yes, Rolan Ras-Erkéltis. You and I, and Tayon, we have felt the weight of grief, perhaps we are the only ones here who have. I mourn for your brother as well, and for what may happen to you. Sit back down, Rolan, and I will try to explain."

Rolan watched him for another moment with squinted eyes, then returned to his seat. The Taennishman faced him as the last light of the sun faded and the oarsmen lit torches. But he did not get a chance to answer. There was a swarm of spiraling light from every direction, and Rolan found himself surrounded by unnamable malice.

"*Tfashg'twa! Gruntagkshk!* Beware! Gruntags!" exclaimed several Karjans at once. They dropped the handles to their oars and drew their swords. Rolan stood up and knocked the end off of his *árukand* walking-staff, exposing the hidden blade, but all he could see was a chaos of deformed monsters and weapons glinting in the light. Gleaming metallic serpentines slithered between them. And there was a lot of mist. He felt the rage welling up inside of him again, that deep fury, and again it became like a physical force that he could battle, and he turned to face it. The pale light shone from his eyes and hands, stronger than before, and furious wails ripped from his mouth. He ran at the seething mass of weapons and began slashing and chopping and ripping at everything with his sword and with his claws. Something grabbed him from behind and held him tight so that he could not move; he struggled and writhed and screamed like a monster and began to kick and rip at it with his exposed toenails. His mind was a blank of cold furry and he could feel sweat pouring out of him and falling onto the floor of the boat, steaming and bubbling like acid. The thing holding him jerked him around to face it, and he cried out and tried to bite and slash it with his teeth; then he saw that he was staring into the face of Hanroy.

"Don't attack them!" Hanroy screamed above Rolan's yowls. "Whatever you do, don't attack anything now! They are already gone! Rolan! Are you there? Can you hear me? Can you understand me? Don't attack anything! They want you to attack! They want you to fight! But you must not! You must be still!"

Rolan screamed and kicked and tried to bite. Hanroy shook him.

"Stop, Rolan! Stop! You must not fight now! Do you hear me? You must not fight! *You are becoming a grosk*, Rolan! That is the deep venom of the grosk! That is what Nammar was going to tell you! Stop fighting! Now!"

Rolan was still. The fury vanished, the pale light went out. Hanroy let go. Rolan sank to the floor of the boat with a whimper, dropped his sword at his side. The monsters were gone.

"Is anybody hurt?" he wheezed.

"No, Rolan, no." Hanroy replied with a relieved sigh. "The gruntags ambushed us. They were waiting by the riverbank. One of them had a flaysword again. They attacked with flyfires. But I don't think they were expecting to meet a Taennishman. Nammar stopped them. Nobody was hurt. This time I'm sure they won't be back."

Sometime later in the night, when the pallid moon was high in the sky, Rolan awoke feverish. He shivered in the damp air; the others eyed him briefly and continued their rowing. There was a conversation going on behind him, a conversation of deep and worried voices.

"We can't do it now, on the boat," said one voice, S'Tam, apparently. Another voice, probably Honroy, agreed. "You might kill him."

"We'll have to," replied another voice. "Dog feathers, we can't wait another day... Nammar, what would you say?"

"The venom of the grosk continues to work its evil." said a fourth voice, somewhat calmer and graver than the others. "There is a protection around the boat now, but the gruntags may attack again, even if they can't get in. There was something else too – I think you saw them, Tayon – *mordhs*. The sight of any of them may cause Rolan to react again..."

Tayon's voice interrupted. "Yes, I saw the mordhs. Cat feathers! This is a grave portent. I have not seen them active like that since they fused into the body of Gashug-Tairanda."

There was a moment of silence, then Nammar continued. "You saw what happened when they attacked! I'm afraid that the decision of what to do it is not ours. But I am afraid of the consequences."

"So, then..." said S'Tam. "We do it?"

The other three voices, no, there were seven or eight voices now, agreed. There was a heavy sigh from one or more of them. The first voice said again, "Nammar, can your *lumáaris* make him sleepy?"

"I cannot use the *lumáaris* like that, and he's not mine; you know that. He uses *me*. And he has chosen to be silent in this matter; because we all know what is best to do."

"Then I'll use the *némurath* tea." said Hanroy. There was the sound of groping carefully, and then less carefully, through a pack. "Here," Hanroy said. "Now, are we all agreed on this? And Tayon, do you want to try the illusion stone?"

There was silence, then sounds of reluctant agreement.

Tayon approached Rolan from out of the night. "Oh, Rolan, you are awake. Swords and daggers! I think you've been awake and listening the whole time! How much have you heard? Well, never mind, I'll tell you what is happening. You heard Hanroy explain that the venom of the *ghrosk* is turning you into a *ghrosk*

172

yourself." (He pronounced "grosk" with a menacing, "red" coloring.) "Those gruntags have a *mechana*, we think, which they use to 'open' a *mechana* that the grosk put into you when it stung you. That *mechana* is embedded in your flesh, probably in your side, where you were stung. Each time it is 'opened', it releases venom that affects you.

"The Ancients knew that deep within each living body there is a spiral of life; it is very small but it determines what, and to some extent, who, we are. They made *mechana*s to affect this spiral of life, originally to correct problems such as deformities. But part of their fall was that they chose to tamper with this part of nature, this part that was created by Teilyándal' near the dawn of time. Grosks were first made with such tampering, though they were in imitation of what the Karjans call *Lijnan-Kwarhmaki* – one of their most dog-featheredly gruesome concepts. The monster Gaeshug-Tairánda was made in the same manner, as are all of its minions such as grosks, and now, we have learned, gruntags, and mordhs. And there are others as well.

"One of these *mechana*s has been placed inside your body. This is how you are becoming a grosk. Nammar and Hanroy and Andri and S'Tam and I have decided to try to remove it. Here, before we get to Hwatsats Hondrakch. If we try to go ashore, we will be ambushed by the gruntags. If we wait until we get there, where you can be taken care of better, you may already have faded. By faded, I mean you may be dead;

your body may have become a grosk. Grosks and gruntags and so on are all counterfeits; they seem alive but they are not; they are manufactured. They have the spiral of life, but they do not have the Breath of Life that Teilyándal' puts into living things. If you become a grosk, you yourself will die, though your corpse will still be animated." He paused, as if to let Rolan feel the horror of the situation.

"So we will try to remove the *mechana* here, and you will be taken care of when we get to Hwatsats Hondrakch. But first I must ask; do you wish for us to do it? There is a chance you may die in the process."

Rolan shivered. His eyes were going blank, probably from the fever, which was growing noticeably worse. And there was that deep rage within his heart again, he could not name it, but he knew that it was there to destroy him. He looked at his hand (what he could see of it through his half-blind eyes) and saw that the blackish-green patch was much larger, covering most of the back of his hand and running down one finger, down to an elongated claw.

"Will... this be gone?" he asked. "If you remove it, will my hand be... normal again?"

"We don't know, Rolan. But the change will stop, at least."

Rolan sighed. For a hideous moment the fury raised up into his mind and he tried to strike at Tayon, who grabbed him. Then it was gone, as if it never had been. He sat back down and shuddered again. That wrath was the mind of a grosk, he told himself.

"Yes, do it." he said after a long silence, then he added, "...and, if... if I die, there is a statue of a Karjan warrior in my pack. Arnul... Arnul liked it. If I die, find him and give it to him."

"Yes, Rolan. Hanroy or I will do that. ...We will remove the evil *mechana* now. Hanroy, do you have that *némurath* tea ready?"

"Yes, coming." said a voice in the darkness. Hanroy approached, gave Rolan a cup of the tea. He sipped at it, found it familiar from his childhood but much stronger and very bitter. He frowned.

"It won't taste good," said Hanroy, "but drink it and you will go to sleep and not feel when we try to remove the *mechana*."

Rolan sipped some more. Tayon brought out a small, round, pinkish-grey stone from his pocket, and held it before Rolan's eyes. "This is an illusion stone," he stated. "I have planned an illusion with it, which will show you my tale. That must all be told, if ever you are fight against Gaeshug-Tairánda and rescue your brother. For I am the Tayon Dar-Táeminos of which you have heard. I am the forger of the Circle of Shining, and yes, I was, in a way, destroyed by its powers. I am the one who caused the creation of Gaeshug-Tairánda. That must all be told. Do you wish to see the tale while we remove the *mechana*? Some parts of it are very frightening. Do you wish to see it?"

"Yes." was all that Rolan could say; the tea was already taking effect. He lay down on the bench in the boat while the rowers kept up their incessant rhythm.

He felt Tayon place the illusion stone near him, and his vision opened up into a new and strange scene. The terror of the grosk lifted from him as he slipped into a different world, and he prepared to watch what was to be shown to him.

To be continued in Book II, "The Wanderer".

APPENDIXES

STEVEN E. SCRIBNER

APPENDIX I:
SPELLING AND PRONUNCIATION

Tondish words are not originally written with English letters, so I have attempted to transliterate them. The system of spelling I have chosen is systematic; using it, most people can pronounce all of the words as correctly as possible given their non-Tondish accents.

However, the spelling system it is not exactly English; it is the system used for spelling words "borrowed" from many languages *into* English. It will be familiar to anyone who has studied Japanese, Indonesian, Turkish, Hawaiian, Russian, Navajo, etc., as well as invented languages such as Esperanto.

CONSONANTS
Basically, pronounce all of the consonants as in English except:

BH – like a V, but pronounced with both lips.

CH – always as in "church", not as in "school".

DH – like the TH in "them".

GH – like a very soft or 'voiced' German/Scottish CH; heard in the "correct" pronunciation of *Afghanistan*. Note: This sound figures in several words in Fyorian, collectively called "red" words (see glossary for an explanation).

H – always as in "hat", even at the end of a word.

HL – a difficult sound, at least for the speaker of English. It occurs in various languages, such as Navajo (spelled Ł), Welsh (spelled LL), several African languages, and some dialects of Chinese. Basically, it is a "voiceless" or "breathy" L, made by putting one's tongue in the position to say an L and then saying a TH instead, without changing the position of the tongue. Fortunately for speakers of English, this sound occurs (in Tond) only in Karjanic, and therefore in few words used in this book.

HM, HN, HNG – this is a trio of very difficult Karjanic sounds, known to linguists as "aspirated voiceless nasals". To pronounce them, say an N, M, or NG (the latter as in "singer"), but precede the sound with an H – which (if you do it correctly) blends with the M, N, or NG to produce a puff of breath through the nose.

J – always as in "judge".

KH – the CH sound in German *doch*, Scottish *loch*, or the "correct" pronunciation of *"Chanukkah"* (compare GH). In Fyorian, this sound is pronounced very smoothly and with no hint of a "rasp"; in Karjanic it is a little rougher. Note: This sound figures in several words in Fyorian, collectively called "red" words (see glossary for an explanation).

NG – always as in "singer", even at the beginning of a word. Not as in "finger" or "danger".

PH – like an F, but pronounced with both lips.

Q – in Tondish languages, this letter stands for a click made with the tongue behind the teeth – the sound sometimes rendered "tsk" in American comics. This sound occurs in Fyorian, but is much more common in Drennic.

TH – always as in "thin", not as in "them". Compare DH.

TS – as in "cats", even at the beginning of a word (like Z in German or ツ in Japanese, if you are familiar with either of those languages).

X – in Tondish languages, this letter stands for a click made in the back of the mouth; a deep "catch" in the throat, similar to ع in Arabic, if you are familiar with that language. This sound is particularly strong in Fyorian, where it is often pronounced with an audible "pop" from the back of the throat. This sound does not exist in Karjanic.

Y – always a consonant, so the beginning of Fyorian sounds like the beginning of "fjord".

ZH – the Z in "azure" and/or the S in "vision".

' – the apostrophe is usually used to designate a glottal stop (a brief "catch" in the back of the throat, as in some Cockney pronunciations of "bottle"; not nearly as severe as X). Sometimes, however, it is used to separate consonants that would otherwise blend together: *S'Tai* does not sound like "sty", and *bad'hani* contains a D followed by an H, not a DH sound (see above). See the glossary if there are any questions about this point in individual words. Finally, it may be used to indicate sounds that are dropped: *Teilyándal'* is short for *Teilyándala*.

Note that in Fyorian, certain consonant sounds (particularly L, N, and R) can be pronounced "double", that is, drawn out to twice as long as normal. Thus, *kullándu* sounds almost as if it were two words in English, "cool LAHNdoo". These three consonants may sound this way because they can also act as vowels (see below).

Also, it is worth noting that the P sound exists in neither Fyorian nor Shervanya; Fyorian lacks the B sound as well (except among "learned" speakers).

VOWELS

Basically:

A as in "father" (or in Karjanic, as in "raw" if you pronounce this differently); AA is the same but more drawn-out or exaggerated; AE is the A in "bad" (so the monster is *GASH-ug-Tairánda*, not *GAY-shug*); AI as in "haiku"

E as in "pet"; EI as in "eight"

I as in "pit"; II is the I in "ski" or the EE in "feet"

O as in "go" (but without the closing of the lips at the end); OO as in "hook"

U has two sounds:

In Fyorian and most other Tondish languages, U sounds like the OO in "too", with no trace of a Y at the beginning, and is barely sounded at the end of words.

In Karjanic, U sounds as in "duck".

Y is not used as a vowel.

The accent mark (á, é, etc.) does not change the sound or volume (stress) of the vowel; it merely indicates a higher voice-pitch for the syllable in which it occurs. In Drennic, a tonal language, there are several types of "accent marks", designating pitch contours of individual syllables.

Note that in Fyorian and Shervanya, two closely related languages, L, N, and R may be used as vowels. The L, used in this way, resembles the "LE" at the end of English words such as "apple" or "bottle". The R resembles the vowel sound in "her" or "bird". The N is somewhat problematic: basically it resembles the N in "didn't" but may sound closer to an M or NG depending on what sound follows it (compare the N in the English word "think"). If you speak Japanese, it's easier to think of it as the ン sound rather than anything in English.

ANGLICIZATION

Pronunciation of all Tondish words follows the rules enumerated above, except these four:

Tond and *grosk* sound out exactly as if they were English words (Fyorian *tánd* and *grásku*).

Kaii rhymes with "Hawaii", though without the "catch" in the throat used in some pronunciations.

Mechana is a coined English word, derived from the beginning of "mechanical", which it sounds like: *Meh-CAN-nuh* (it would be spelled *mekáena* if it were spelled in the manner of other Tondish words).

Note also that several of the names of major characters in the story have been anglicized for ease of reading. Thus, there is Rolan instead of *Ró'lan* (pronounced Roe-lahn, not Role-ahn), Arnul instead of *Árnll*, Shillayne instead of *Shiléin*, Tayon instead of

Téyan, Nammar instead of *Náemar*, and Ai-Leena instead of Ailíina.

All of these words and names are spelled out in the glossary as in an English dictionary, should any questions arise.

APPENDIX II:
GLOSSARY OF TONDISH WORDS

(Note: although detailed explanations of many words are given here, the etymologies of compound Karjanic words are generally too complex to give in this short overview.   They will be found in the forthcoming auxiliary volume, A Guide to Tond.)

ádhel: (AH-thel, TH as in "them")   A type of Fyorian outer robe, tied with a rope around the waist.

ahíinor: (ah-HEE-nor)   A Fyorian loremaster.   (Fyorian, root *ahíinu*, the loremasters' art.)

ahíinu: (ah-HEE-noo)   The Fyorian loremasters' art. Often   translated   as   "lore",   *ahíinu*   includes knowledge of ancient tales (true "lore") and use of *mechana*s   [see]   as   well   as   medicine   and psychology.   Much   *ahíinu*   works   by   means   of physical   (mechanical,   chemical,   electronic,   and quantum)   phenomena,   though   this   is   often obscured by complex layers of symbolism and the apparently "magic" nature of the *mechanas*. There are four types or styles of *ahíinu*, called *ii-yam*, *ter-yam*, *ren-yam*, and *fyer-yam* (first, second, etc.), labeled in ascending order of difficulty and possibility of danger.

Ai-Leena, Ailíina: (eye-LEE-na) Sherványa feminine name, the name of the half-Sherványa queen of the Tower of Dawn. Also, a Sherványa musical mode, corresponding (roughly) to the notes E, F#, G, B, C, E and the "attendant" eighth-tones, the third mode of the evening during the Nocturnal Music. (Sherványa "beautiful stars", akin to Fyorian *áru lénn*.)

Ancients, the: The people who lived before the Devastation, the makers of the *mechanas*. (Fyorian *fyúralan*, old ones.)

árukand: (AH-roo-kahnd) A walking-staff, an essential item for the wandering *ahíinor* loremaster; particularly, such a staff with a hidden sword. (Fyorian "a thing used for walking", from *árukas*, to walk.)

avalinkáalei: (ah-vah-ling-KAH-lay) A Sherványa musical mode, consisting (roughly) of the notes C, E, F, G, B, C, and their "attendant" eighth-tones; the second mode of the evening during the Nocturnal Music. (Sherványa "wandering of the moon".)

áyushaa: (EYE-yoo-shah) A kind of dry bread eaten on journeys, very nutritious but not particularly tasty.

(Sherványa 'bread for walking', akin to Fyorian *áruku-shái*.)

Ázugh, blade of: (AH-zugh, the GH sounds like a very soft or "voiced" German CH) A *mechana* (see), similar to the Fiery Eye knife, which can be made to show pre-made illusions, telling stories. (Fyorian; the meaning of "*ázugh*" is uncertain, but may be based either on *ázurghas* "to be caught up [in a story]" or Karjanic *Lijnan-'Adzuk* [see].)

Battle Srogat: (s'roe-gawt) The drug *srogat* (see) as used by the Karjan *tsajuk* warriors for battle. (Karjanic *bad'hani srokat.*)

Blue-green words: In the Fyorian language, some words containing the palatal LY and NY sounds are said to be *áwas ke teln* ("blue-green words") or *kéwan teln* ("water-colored words"), and are assumed to have pleasant meanings. These sounds may be playfully inserted into other words or names to make them seem more pleasant (this was originally a poetic device). Interestingly, in the third century after the Devestation, Fyorian philosopher Rónya Dar-Áldisar tried to correlate the "blue-greenness" with the pleasant aspects of *Kewándii* (see), though this idea was never fully developed. (See *red words.*)

Borrogg: (bor-awg-'g) The land in the northeast part of Tond, surrounded by mountains. Considered to be the land of evil in several Tondish mythologies. (Karjanic.)

187

Chákreh: (CHAH-kreh) The second largest city on the island of Ond, site of the Ondish royal palace. (from Karjanic *ts'hakreh*, "palace".)

Chashk: (chawsh'k) A Karjan-like people living on seven islands near and within the Drellyan States.

Chelloi: The (title of the) Drennic loremaster.

chud: A mutation occurring in the Karjans; reddish or magenta irises, which supposedly give one much greater night vision. The color is greatly prized in the Imperium, particularly among the *tsajuk* warriors, where it is the most common. (Karjanic *ch'hud*.)

Circle of Shining: see Shining, Circle of.

Devastation, the: The great destruction of the old Fyorian empire. (Fyorian *mordhándu tókaa*, "great destruction time".)

Drakhnar: (drawkh-nar, the KH sounds like a German CH) A gold coin of the Karjan Imperium, equal to one hundred silver *bvraktuk*. (Karjanic, plural of *trakhnar*.)

Drellyan States: The confederation of the Drellyan Islands.

Drellyan: (DRELL-yun) The Islands north of the Drennic Islands. Also the people who live there (they are closely related to the Drenn), and their language, considered by some to be a dialect of Drennic.

Drenn: (dren-'n) (A member of) the race of people traditionally living on the many islands in the northwest of Tond. They usually have light brown skin (often with an unusual grayish tinge), brown eyes and blondish- or reddish-brown hair. (They call themselves *Dreün'n*, said with a descending voice-pitch.)

Drennic Islands: The (southern half of the) archipeligo in northwest Tond, home of the Drenn.

Drennic Lands: The northwest shore of Tond, near the Drennic Islands, one homeland of the Drenn. Also called "Drennlands".

Drennic: The tonal language of the Drenn, distantly related to Fyorian, and actually consisting of about fifty mutually unintelligible dialects. (The Drenn call their language *Dwen Dreün'n*, said with a high then a descending voice-pitch.)

Drennlands: see Drennic Lands.

Earth Proper: The region of planet Earth on this side of the tesseract to Tond; the familiar world in which we live.

Ei Eyuhand: (AY Ay-yoo-hahnd) The name of an oasis in west Rohándal. (Fyorian; the meaning of *Ei* is uncertain, *eyuhand* means "oasis".)

Emb: (Emb, the B is not silent.) The people living in the south of Tond, who originated outside of Tond. They usually have dark skin, hair, and eyes. Also, the language of these people, not related to any Tondish language. (They are called Emb by other peoples in Tond; the name is not considered pejorative though it is actually a misreading of the beginning of Archaic Fyorian *mbálan*, "southerners". They call themselves either Emb or

Mérksa, and their language either Emb or Mérksayiis.)

Enkéilii: (eng-KAY-lee) Spirits of light created near (or before) the beginning of time; angels. (Old Fyorian.)

Eshwaa: (ESH-wah) Shar [see].

Éyuhand: (Ay-yoo-hond) An oasis, particularly one in the desert of Rohándal. (Fyorian, "green place".

First Sundering: See Sunderings, the.

Fiery Eye: A type of *ahíinu* [see], a fire which produces images, showing scenes of things happening far away. Also, **Fiery Eye knife**: the *mechana* used to make the Fiery Eye, usually shaped like a short, blunt knife.

floater: A form of life which is unique to Tond. Organisms with large gas-filled "balloons" (either single blimp-shaped, or double- or triple-lobed) which expand and float into the air during the day (to avoid predators and drift to a new location) and contract at night, lowering the Floater to the ground to put out roots and take nourishment from the soil. Despite their size (they can be up to twenty meters in diameter), floaters are probably related to fungi. (Fyorian *dányala*, "that which floats", from *dányas*, to float.)

flyfire: A type of *ahíinu* (see), an energy field which can be used to surround someone or something and fly it to another location. Also, **flyfire crystal**: the *mechana* used to make the flyfire, usually shaped like a thumbnail-sized red crystal.

Four, the: The "four elements": fire, water, earth ("stone" in the Tondish version), and air; important in the lore of the Fyorians.

fyer-yam: (f'yair-yahm.) The "fourth level" of Fyorian *ahíinu*, consisting of the use of certain extremely powerful *mechana*s, and forbidden by the *ahíinor* because of its destructive potential. (Fyorian *fyer-yam [ahíinu]*, fourth type of [lore].)

Fyorian: (the beginning is like the beginning of FJORD.) (A member of) the race of people traditionally living in Rohándal and surrounding areas. They usually have light brown skin, brown eyes, and blond or light brown hair. Also, the language of these people, an important lingua franca and one of the great literary languages of Tond. (The Fyorian people call themselves *fyoránya* and their language *fyorándii*.)

Gaejtark-Bad'hani: (gadge-tark bawd-haw-nee) In Karjan mythology, the war-god; the builder of empires and destroyer of imperfect things; also the instigator of violence. Its symbol is the eagle. (Karjanic, ultimately from the roots *katark*, to make, *pat'han*, war.)

Gaejtark-Kwarhmaki: (gadge-tark quar-h'maw-kee) The Karjanic concept of radical transformation; internal enlightenment leading to outward beauty; or giving help or healing to another. Its symbol is the caterpillar changing into a butterfly. See *Lijnan-Kwarhmaki*. (Karjanic, ultimately from the roots *katark*, to make, *kwarhmak*, change.)

Gaeshug-Tairánda: (GASH-ug-tye-RAHN-duh) A powerful shape-shifting monster created by Roagh the Karjan in an attempt to rule all of Tond. (Karjanic *gaeshug*, attrocities, plural of *kaeshug* + Fyorian "nameless evil": *tai*, *táyu*, evil, *ro*, without, *ánda*, name.)

Gánuwein: (GAHN-oo-wayne) The major city on the island of Ond. The name refers (in Ondish) to oak trees, which grow there in profusion.

Glephadhi: (gleh-PHAW-thee; the PH is an F pronounced with both lips) A people of unknown origin, perhaps related to the Karjans but speaking a language closer to Tondish languages such as Fyorian (but with a number of non-Tondish features). They generally have black hair, blue or green eyes and light skin, like the Karjans, but tend to be shorter and stockier. Their original home was on the banks of the River Cheihar, but they fled an attempted genocide by the Karjans, and now live in scattered villages in both the far north and the far south of Tond. (*Glephadhi* is their name for themselves; other Tondish peoples often call them *Glefánya*, their Fyorian name.)

glow-ball: A common loremasters' *mechana*; an apparently metallic ball which can be "suspended" above the ground and "opened" to produce light. (Fyorian *lámu-o*, "glow-ball".)

Grand srakah: A sub-style of *srakah* music (see) played very loudly on drums, low tuned gongs and bass marimba. Many of the lowest ("grandest") notes are felt rather than heard.

grosk: A kind of monster associated with Gaeshug-Tairánda; twice the size of a man, having a huge alligator-like jaw and a poisonous sting in its tail, and covered with green-grey, semi-metalic, organic toothy armor. Often manufactured by Gaeshug-Tairánda by mutating a living being (usually a human) by means of a *mechana* which alters the "spiral of life" (see), in imitation of the transformations associated with Lijnan-Kwarhmaki (see). (Fyorian "deformity" [*grásku*, the final U is barely sounded]. A very similar word meant "servant" in an older dialect of Karjanic, as grosks are servants of Gaeshug-Tairánda. The word was probably coined, and emphasized that the "servants" were not human; *krosok* meant "a person who serves" [verb *krozoka*, "to serve"], but *krosko* [plural *grosko*] meant "a thing which serves".)

gruntag: see *gruntagkshk*.

gruntagkshk, gruntagkchk: (grun-tag-k'sh-k, grun-tag-k'ch-k) Gruntags; one of Gaeshug-Tairanda's two armies, the manufactured creatures that appear to be monstrous, nonsensical combinations of miscellaneous parts of other creatures and objects. (Karjanic "manufactured creatures", ultimately from roots *krutak*, creature, *kochok*, to manufacture.)

háru-kándis: (HAH-roo-KAHN-diss) A game, similar to chess, but with two to four players, each playing a different "kingdom". (Fyorian "Battling Kingdoms": *háru*, battling [adjective form of *háras*, to battle], *kándis*, kingdoms [pl. of *kándu*].)

hragezhi tsegaltsekk: (h'raw-geh-zsheet-seh-kawlt-seck-'k.) The "Imperial Script", the flowing, vertical form of writing the Karjanic language. (Karjanic "royal style of writing", from *hrakezh*, royalty [see], *tsekal*, to write, -*tsekk*, type of.)

hrakezh: (h'raw-kezsh.) (A member of) the Karjan royalty.

hutark: (huh-tark) (A member of) the Karjan priesthood.

hwatsats: (h'wawt-sawts) (The stone tower in the center of) a Karjan city-state in the Imperium.

Hwatsats Hondrakch: (h'wawt-sawts hone-draw-k'ch) "Tower of Dawn", a *hwatsats* (see) in the eastern part of the Karjan Imperium. (Karjanic *hwatsats*, "tower", *Hondrakch*, "sun which is approaching us", "sunrise", from *hatrak*, "sun".)

Hwatsats Ragezhi: See Kings, Tower of.

ii-yam: (ee-yahm) The "first level" of Fyorian *ahíinu*, consisting mostly of memorized histories and legends. (Fyorian *ii-yam [ahíinu]*, first type [of lore]).

káhei: (KAH-hay) Coffee.

Kaii: (rhymes with HAWAII.) The forested northern region of Tond, home of the Kayánti.

Karghoul: see *kargurtstk*.

kargurtstk: (kar-goort-st'-k) Karghouls; one of the armies of Gaeshug-Tairánda, humanoid reptiles, "lizard men". (Karjanic "killer man-lizards", a coined word ultimately from the roots *kar*, man [as in Karjan], *kool* [pl. *gool*], lizard, *tsatak*, to kill.)

Karjanic: (kar-JAN-ic) The language of the Karjans.

Karjans: (Kar-jan) The people whole live in the Imperium and surrounding areas, between Rohándal and the Emb Lands. They generally are taller and slimmer than other Tondish peoples, have dark hair, light skin, and blue or green eyes (or "eyes of *chud*", [see]). They originated outside of Tond and arrived by ship, settling along the river Cheihar, first as conquerors (the Old Imperium under Tarshkn) and later as friends of the *ahíinor*. (Karjanic, the word is actually an adjective form of *karchaen*, "people", from *kar* "man" + *chaen* "woman".)

Kavezán: (kah-veh-ZAHN) The Fyorian and Shervanya pronunciation of *Hwatsats* (see); the word probably entered the Shervanya language through Ondish (which changes H to K under certain conditions).

Kayánti: (kye-YAHN-tih) (A member of) the race of people traditionally living in the north of Tond, in Kaii and surrounding areas. They usually have light brown skin (sometimes with an unusual grayish tinge), brown eyes, and brown hair. Also, the language of these people, distantly related to

Fyorian. (They call themselves *Kayánta* and their language *Kayánti*.)

Kayef Grechdaemwosh Arjala!: (Kye-yeff gretch-dam-w'sh ar-jaw-law) The old battle-cry of the Karjan Imperium under the rule of Tarshkn. The phrase is translated as "We come to conquer", but is actually much stronger, meaning roughly "In a never-ending process, we come to destroy all of you who are inferior to us, and your complete obliteration is beneficial to you". (See "The Languages of Tond" in the auxiliary volume for a more complete explanation.)

Kelsíima: (kel-SEE-muh) Another name for Old Fyorian, the language spoken by the Ancients.

Kétatang: (KET-uh-tong) An extremely resonant frame drum with metal jingles. (Fyorian, onomatopoeic.)

Kewándii: (keh-WAHN-dee) Fyorian personification of the element Water and "the flow", also associated with blood and, metaphorically, with time (which is considered to flow.)

Kings, Tower of: A *hwatsats* (see) on the banks of the River Cheihar near the Great Lake Tsenwakh, eastern Karjan Imperium. The tower was destroyed by the monster Gaeshug-Tairánda. (Karjanic *Hwatsats Ragezhi*; *hwatsats* "tower", *ragezhi*, adjective-form plural of *hrakezh*, "royalty".)

kitál: (kih-TALL) A stringed musical instrument, resembling a hammered dulcimer but played by plucking or strumming. (origin uncertain; the instrument is popular throughout Tond.)

Kullándu: (kool-LAHN-doo) Fyorian personification of the element Fire, also associated with power, creativity, procreation, and destruction.

Law, Sword of: The greatest of the *mechana*s, of Taennish origin, unlike the others. The Sword was capable of reading a man's soul and giving punishment according to his intent in whatever matter for which he was being judged. The Sword is considered to have been lost in the Devastation. (Fyorian *túas ke máltus*, "Sword of Law".)

Light, Master of: The (title of the) leader of the loremasters' order in Rohándal. (Fyorian *lúmukor*.)

Lijnan-'Adzuk: (lidge-nawn awd-zuk) In Kajanic mythology, the evil deity of corruption by words: temptation, persuasion, propaganda. Its symbol is the jabbering monkey. (Karjanic, ultimately from the roots *linan*, to destroy or corrupt, *hatsuk*, to speak in a tempting or persuasive manner.)

Lijnan-Kwarhmaki: (lidge-nawn quar-h'maw-kee) In Karjanic mythology, the evil deity of radical transformation; internal corruption leading to outward ugliness; or change, deformity, or injury visited upon another against their will. Its symbol is the snake shedding its skin. (Karjanic, ultimately from the roots *linan*, to destroy or corrupt, *kwarhmak*, change.)

lizard-man: See *kargoortstk*.

Lore: See *ahíinu*.

Lornáalis: (lor-NAHL-iss) Fyorian personification of the element Air, also associated with emotions and the imagination. (The root *lor-* or *lorn-* appears in a number of Fyorian words for air, sky, up, etc.; + -*áalis* "all of")

Lumáaris: (loo-MAR-is) A spirit of light, said to come from Teilyándal' (see), with which Taennishmen communicate when it appears. (Fyorian, 'group of lights', from its outward appearance, though many cannot see it.)

Lúmukor: See Light, Master of.

Lurker: A genus of carnivorous marsupial (five species) found in the northern mountains of Tond. Lurkers are known for their habit of (as their name implies) waiting out of sight, sometimes under man-made structures such as bridges, and then suddenly jumping out and attacking their prey – bears, dogs, and other large mammals including humans. Armed with sharp fangs and claws, they can walk on either two legs (like a human) or all four. Two species sport a turtle-like shell, though they are much more flexible and fast-running. (Fyorian *wártala*, 'that which lurks', from *wártas*, 'to lurk or hide for ambush'.)

Maellórn: (mal-LORN) Fyorian name for the moon.

mechanas: Strange objects left over from the Ancients, and used by the Fyorian loremasters. Each *mechana* does a specific thing, often unrelated to its appearance, and some may only be used a specific number of times. (A coined English word, related to "machine" or "mechanical". The Fyorian word is *ahíinand* "a thing used for *ahíinu* [the loremasters art]".)

mordh: (morth, pronounce the TH as in "them".) A *mordhándala* (see).

mordhándala, mordhándalan: (mor-DHAHN-dah-luh. The DH is like the TH in THEM) The serpent-like creatures from another world which are trying to destroy Tond, and which are the source of all the evil of Gaeshug-Tairánda, the gruntagkshk, etc. (Fyorian, "that which destroys": *mordhándala*, "that [living being] which destroys, from *mordhándu* "[great] destruction".)

némurath: (NEM-oo-rahth) A relaxing tea made from a plant of the same name, and drunk by Fyorians (particularly children) at bedtime. Extremely high doses can be used as an anesthetic, even in adults, though this is not a well-known fact. (Fyorian "sleep herb": *némas*, to sleep, *rath*, herb.)

Nocturnal Music: Quiet music played by Sherványa musicians to help others sleep. In some Sherványa cities and villages, nocturnal music lasts all night, and all citizens must play when their turn comes.

Old Fyorian: The language spoken by the Ancients. Also called *Kelsíima*.

Ond: An island in the Great Lake Tsenwakh in the eastern Karjan Imperium, home of the Ondish.

Ond, Five Mountains of: The five high peaks comprising the backbone of the island of Ond.

Ondish: The people living on the island of Ond, of mixed Fyorian and Karjanic ancestry. Also, the language of these people, closely related to Fyorian but containing several hundred commonly used Karjanic words. (The Ondish call themselves *Andánya* and their language *Andándi*.)

Outer Tond: The world of Tond outside of Taennishland, so called by the Taennishmen.

pshakat: (p'shaw-kawt) A drug derived from a secret plant, which induces intense pain, dread, despair, and nightmarish hallucinations. Used as a form of torture by Karjans. (Karjanic.)

red words: In the Fyorian language, some words containing the GH and KH sounds are said to be *rúas ke teln* ("red words") or *kúlas ke teln* ("fire-colored words"), and, with the exception of grammar words like *gháan* ("I would"), are assumed to have unpleasant meanings. These sounds may be playfully inserted into other words or names to make them seem darker or less pleasant – this was originally a poetic device. The concept is similar to "salty" or "four-letter" words in English, though Fyorian "red words" are not necessarily explatives. Interestingly, in the third century after the Devestation, Fyorian philosopher Rónya Dar-Áldisar tried to correlate the "redness" with the unpleasant aspects of *Kullándu* (see), though this idea was never fully developed. (See *blue-green words*.)

ren-yam: (ren-yahm) The "third level" of Fyorian *ahíinu*, consisting of the use of the Ancients' *mechana*s. (Fyorian *ren-yam [ahíinu]*, third type [of lore].)

Rohándal: (ro-HAHN-dahl) The desert home of the Fyorians; the land south of Kaii and north of the Karjan Imperium. (Fyorian "no-place land" [=desert]: *ro*, without, *hand[u]*, place, *-dal*, place-name ending.)

sánatar sauce: (SAHN-a-tar.) A sweet sauce made from two types of berries; often used as a marinade for meats. (Fyorian "two berries", dual form of *sánatu*, berry.)

séntem: (SEN-tem) a small hand-held glockenspiel. (Fyorian, onomatopoeic.)

Séyar Eyuhand: (SAY-yar Ay-yoo-hahnd) The name of an oasis in east Rohándal. ("Two Hills Oasis": *séyar*, dual of *sei*, 'hill', *eyuhand* means 'oasis'.)

Shankál': A stance in Fyorian fencing: knees slightly bent, body tensed and leaning slightly forward, sword at an angle from which it is easy to both strike and deflect a blow. (Fyorian, "guarded person".)

Shar: Physical manifestation of *Teilyándal'* (see) in Tond. Also called Eshwaa.

Sherványa: (share-VAHN-yuh) (A member of) the race of people traditionally living in Lánnishar and other eastern areas of Tond. They usually have light brown skin, brown or dark brown eyes, and blond hair. Also, the language of these people, closely related to Fyorian, and considered the most musical Tondish language. (They call themselves *Sherványa* and their language *Sherványáal*.)

sheyándol: (shay-YAHN-dole) A Sherványa musical mode, corresponding (roughly) to the notes C, D, F, G, B, C, and their attendant eighth-tones. The first mode of the evening for the Nocturnal Music. (Sherványa 'darkening'.)

Shining, Circle of: A powerful *mechana* forged by Teyan Dar-Táeminos in the Tower of Kings, attempting to substitute for the lost Sword of Law. The Circle was used by Roagh the Karjan to create the monster Gaeshug-Tairánda, and was later used as a deterrent for raiding Karjan warriors and to initiate new members into the order of the Fyorian loremasters. (Fyorian *lumánduaen*, 'shine-light circle', not called by the simpler name 'Circle of Light' [*lúmuaen*] because Teyan did not want it associated too closely with the Master of Light [see].)

skullpox: An infectious disease, related to ebola, and characterized by high fever, vomiting, and blood-filled boils. If treated quickly with fever-reducing herbs, most victims recover within a week or two, though they often are disfigured by pitted scars, the result of having picked at the boils. If not treated, the disease can progress to its late stages, including a rotting of the skin of the face, exposing the skull. This form of the disease is always fatal. (Fyorian *krémukhaa yash*.)

Spirit of the Void: See Void, Spirit of the.

srakah: (s'raw-kaw'h) A type of Karjanic classical music played on percussion. The compositions are composed completely in advance, and there is no improvising; but the players often rearrange, add, or remove sections. (See also Grand Srakah.)

srogat: (s'roe-gawt) A drug made from a secret herb and used by Karjan warriors for battle; it induces a heightened state of aggression while nullifying pain. An overdose of the drug results in a rabid/psychotic state and (self-induced) death of the victim. This was used as a form of execution in the Imperium under Tarshkn.

Star, Tower of the: A Karjan-style tower on the Tashkrian island of Sron. (Karjaneic *Hwatsats Hwelen*, Tashkrian *Kvizats ag-Kweghan*, Chashk *Kfaz Kferanni* "Tower of the Star".)

Sunderings, the: Calamitous events in Tondish mythology/history, separations of things which were originally together. The First Sundering separated man from nature and its Creator *Teilyándal'* (see), as well as rendering nature and the Four (see) corrupt and full of violence. Further Sunderings broke up ethnicities and languages; some versions of the story include a Sundering of male and female. (Fyorian *étaghwis*, plural of *étaghu*, 'a case of being broken apart', from *étaghas* 'to be broken apart', related to *etághas*, 'to break apart'.)

Swallow a Whole Mango: A fyorian expression meaning "Be quiet"; an image of something bulky in one's throat hindering speech (even if the Fyorian mangoes are the smaller, yellow variety). Usually stated informally (*"yálu gámúnggá"*), the expression is sometimes rendered ironically as a polite request (*"Kein yálas 'e gám múnggas"*).

Sword of Law: See Law, Sword of.

Taennishland: (TAN-nish) A 'magical' city which moves; home of the Taennish Folk. (partial translation of Fyorian *Táenn nel tánd[u]*.)

Taennishmen, Taennish Folk: (TAN-nish) A mysterious race of people, apparently immortal, and wielding an unknown type of power (which they say does not actually exist). They have appeared many times as wanderers and prophets in Tondish history. Their eyes are of a color not normally visible, but their other features are variable. (Partial translation of Fyorian *Taennánya*.)

talwehéinaa: (tall-weh-HAY-nuh) The Fyorian alphabet. (Fyorian "group of letters", from *talweh[u]*, an archaic word for writing.)

Tarshkn, Tarshk'n: (Tarsh-k'n) The name of the prophet of Gaejtark-Bad'hani and ruler of the Karjan Imperium during its most warlike phase.

Tandáalis: (tahn-DAHL-iss) Fyorian personification of the element Earth or Stone, also associated with steadfastness, hence, knowledge and faith. (The Fyorians, a desert people, have no concept such as "mother earth".) (Fyorian, "all earth", from *tand[u]*, earth.)

Tashkrian: (tawsh-kree-un) A Karjan-like people living on four islands near the Drennic Islands.

Teilyándal': (tay-L'YAHN-dahl, tale-YAHN-dahl.) The Creator, the One who creates to fill the void. The greatest Tondish deity, and God (capital G) in the Fyorian/Taennish monotheistic religion. (Fyorian, short for Teilyándala, "The [good] Creator": from *teilándas*, to create, with the "blue-green" palatalized *L* indicating goodness or pleasantness. See "Blue-green words".)

ten-ball: Tondish billiards. A game played with ten metal, stone, or wooden balls on a table with a concave surface. Some game sets have all ten balls of the same material and size; others have a variety. There is netting around the table; each player tries to use one ball to knock the others out and into his opponent's netting, one point for each ball (minus one point for each ball knocked into his *own* side of the net). The first player with more than seven points wins. If a player can make a ball miss all of the others entirely and drop into his opponent's netting (which is very difficult because of the shape of the table), he replaces all of the opponent's balls, and thus erases all of his opponent's points. (Translated from Fyorian *íinge o*, "ten ball" [the name, like its English translation, is not grammatical; "ten balls" would be *íinge ngas on*].)

ter-yam: (tare-yahm) The "second level" of Fyorian *ahíinu*, consisting of knowledge of medicinal herbs and their uses. (Fyorian *ter-yam [ahíinu]*, second type [of lore].)

Tond: (Rhymes with BOND) A large continent, site of Rohándal, the Karjan Imperium, Kaii, etc. (Fyorian *tand[u]*, land, earth, country.)

Trakesándá!: (trah-keh-SAHN-DAH) "Eat dung!" Considered to be the worst insult in the Fyorian language. To make this expletive even worse, the speaker often states it ironically as a polite request (*"Kein tráku esándas!"*) and rolls the R in the back of the throat, producing a GH-like sound and thus a "red" word (see).

Trálgor: (TRAHL-gor; the first R is rolled in the back of the throat) The devil, the Spirit of the Void [see Void, spirit of]. (Fyorian 'deciever'.)

Trillórn: (tril-LORN) Fyorian name for the sun.

tsajka: (tsawdge-kuh. The TS is like the sound at the end of CATS) A Karjanic curved sword; scimitar. (Ultimately from the same root as *tsajuk*, warrior.)

tsajuk: (tsaw-juck. The TS is like the sound at the end of CATS) A Karjan warrior; also, the caste to which Karjan warriors belong.

tshrakah: (roughly, ch'raw-kaw-'h) A type of Karjanic dance music, based on repeated rhythmic cycles. Each player often composes his own part separately of the others.

T'wadzadz: (roughly, tuh-wawd-zawdz) The ruins of the Tower of Kings in the eastern Karjan Imperium. (Karjanic "those things [i.e. ruins] which until recently were a tower", ultimately from *hwatsats*, "tower".)

Underlord: In the Karjan Imperium, the second in command to the ruling *hrakezh*, usually chosen to be the next ruler after the present one dies. (Karjanic *uzch hrakech* "temporary under-hrakezh").

Void, Spirit of the: Trálgor; the destructive spirit which hates other beings, and deceives or destroys them with the intent of nullifying their existence and returning them (and everything) to the Void, the state of non-creation. (Fyorian *mwáalis ka enkéilii* "spirit or angel of all-nothing".)

Void: The state of nothingness or non-creation, the source of evil in Tond. (Fyorian *mwáalis*, 'all nothing', collective form of *mu*, 'nothing'.)

Wolyáamusei: (Wole-YAH-moo-say) In Sherványa philosophy, the feelings of timidity or fear that a person finds pleasant, because they keep him comfortable and prevent him from going too far into the unknown. Similar to the idea of a "comfort zone". (Sherványa *wo-lyáamusei*, akin to Fyorian *láamas* or *láamu* 'fear', with a 'blue-green' palatal L indicating pleasantness [see *blue-green words*].)

Xóa Éyuhand: (roughly, KO-uh AY-yoo-hond) The name of an oasis in souther Rohándal. (Fyorian; *Xóa* refers to the sound of wind; *Éyuhand* means "oasis".)

Zaman: An little-known ancient incursion into Tond, alluded to in several Tondish mythologies. A couple of ancient Fyorian manuscripts spell the name of this mysterious people Zamanthisk (a combination of sounds not possible in Fyorian or any native Tondish language), indicating that they may have come from outside of Tond – the Karjan continent is usually considered to be a good candidate for their origin.

ABOUT THE AUTHOR

Steven Eric Scribner is a high school teacher, freelance author, blogger, and avant-garde pianist/composer. He graduated from Seattle Pacific University. He has lived in the suburbs of Seattle, in the San Francisco Bay Area, and in Japan. "Tond" is his first novel, though its roots go back more than forty years to imaginary tales he used to invent while walking to and from school. The landscapes in northern Tond (to be seen in Book Two) were inspired by the forests and mountains around Seattle and in Japan, those in Rohándal by eastern Washington State; other aspects of the Tondish world are purely a product of his imagination (though many are symbolic).

Made in the USA
San Bernardino, CA
26 January 2018